# THE LAKERS

James Plumptre, a clergyman in the Church of England, published *The Lakers* in 1798: a comic play gently satirising Lake District tourism and the fashion for botany. Not until 1999 did it receive its first performance, in the Lakeland town of Keswick where the play itself is set. This edition includes annotations identifying the people, places and botanical terms which appear in the play, and a short introduction.

# JAMES PLUMPTRE

# The Lakers:
## A Comic Opera

Edited by B. Wardhaugh

# CONTENTS

# INTRODUCTION

JAMES PLUMPTRE (1771–1832), graduate and fellow
of Clare College, Cambridge and a clergyman in the
Church of England, published his first comic play,
*The Coventry Act*, in 1793, following performances
in Norwich. (Earlier plays, written at school and as
an undergraduate and including a farce and adapta-
tions of Shakespeare, survive in manuscript.) But he
had less success with his next two plays: a tragedy,
*Osway*, was published in 1795 but not performed, and
the same fate befell *The Lakers*, his gentle satire on
British tourism. Written in 1797 at the suggestion
of 'a friend of the Deputy Manager of Covent Garden Theatre', and with specific performers in mind,
it was rejected without comment by that theatre. An
approach to the Haymarket Theatre met with much
the same result. Rather than pursue performance any
further, Plumptre consigned the play 'to the closet',
publishing it at a price of two shillings with a preface
explaining its history.

Despite the title-page designation as an 'opera',
no music was printed with the play, and it seems to
have been supplied to Covent Garden without any.
In at least one case – 'A lady once her lap-dog lost',
in Act I – Plumptre intended to adopt a tune from
another musical play: and, indeed, it would certainly
be feasible to put together a full set of music for *The
Lakers* from the large collection of songs Plumptre

himself edited in 1805.

Despite its reception at Covent Garden and Haymarket, the play is a genuinely funny one, the satire affectionate – Plumptre himself made a series of walking tours around Britain during the 1790s – and its heroine Beccabunga Veronica a splendid creation. *The Lakers* was performed at the Theatre by the Lake in Keswick in 1999, in what seems to have been its first and, so far, only professional production.

The best discussion of Plumptre's life is in Ian Ousby's introduction to his travel journals. Plumptre was from a distinguished family: his father was president of Queen's College, Cambridge, and two of his sisters (he was his parents' tenth child) became known as writers. He married in 1815, and continued to write in a range of genres throughout his life. His output included further plays (collected in a volume in 1818), writings on theatre including a collection of expurgated plays, *The English Drama Purified* (1812), plus sermons, editions of songs and fables, and an edition of *Robinson Crusoe*. A facsimile of the first edition of *The Lakers* was published in 1990, with a brief but helpful introduction, but no annotated edition has previously appeared.

THE EDITOR, Benjamin Wardhaugh, is a Fellow of All Souls College, Oxford. He works on mathematics and science in the seventeenth and eighteenth centuries.

THE TEXT is that of the first edition of 1798. Minor inconsistencies of spacing and italics have been regularized; Plumptre's spelling and punctuation (with the exception of a handful of missing periods) are preserved. Footnotes are the author's; endnotes the editor's. While every effort has been made to trace Veronica's botanical terms and allusions, the editor welcomes notice of any errors or omissions and will be happy to make suitable emendations in a future version of the text. Three pages of advertisements for 'Books ... printed for and sold by W.CLARKE', printed at the end of the original volume, are omitted.

FURTHER READING

James Plumptre, *The Lakers* (Oxford: Woodstock Books, 1990) [a facsimile of the first edition, with an introduction by Jonathan Wordsworth].

Ian Ousby, ed., *James Plumptre's Britain: The journals of a tourist in the 1790s* (London: Hutchinson, 1992).

Anne D. Wallace, *Walking, Literature, and English Culture: The origins and uses of peripatetic in the nineteenth century* (Oxford: Clarendon Press, 1993).

Sam George, *Botany, Sexuality and Women's Writing 1760–1830: From modest shoot to forward plant* (Manchester: Manchester University Press, 2007).

Oxford, January 2009.

# THE
# LAKERS:
## A
# COMIC OPERA,
## IN
# *THREE ACTS.*

—— To Nature's pride,
Sweet KESWICK'S vale, the Muse will guide;
The Muse who trod th'inchanted ground,
Who sail'd the wond'rous Lake around,
With you will haste once more to hail
The beauteous brook of BORROWDALE.

DALTON.°

## London:

PRINTED FOR W. CLARKE, NEW BOND STREET.

1798.

# TO
# TOURISTS
## IN GENERAL,

*But more particularly to those who have taken,*

OR

## INTEND TO TAKE,

THE

# TOUR OF THE LAKES,

IN

*Lancashire, Westmorland, and Cumberland,*

THE FOLLOWING

# OPERA

IS MOST HUMBLY INSCRIBED

BY

THEIR DEVOTED HUMBLE SERVANT,

*THE AUTHOR.*

# PREFACE.

ANY one acquainted with the most popular dramas of the present day will not accuse an author of much vanity, in thinking it no very difficult task to please the public in writing for the stage.

Impressed with this idea, when the Author of the following drama had an offer made him by a friend of the Deputy Manager of Covent Garden Theatre to present any piece, and insure its being, at least, read by him (for pieces are sometimes refused without being read), he immediately set about it; thinking he should be well repaid, if, for a few weeks trouble, he could put a few hundred pounds into his pocket; and that the loss would not be very great if unsuccessful.

To produce a laughable piece, and give the musical composer and scene painter an opportunity of displaying their talents, was the object therefore in writing the following scenes, rather than an attempt at a regular° drama. Yet the Author, in striving to please, did not so far forget his duty as a moralist, as to sacrifice morality to mirth, and good sense to scenery; and while he attempted to amuse, he wished

to expose and lend his feeble aid to correct some of
the follies of the age. He would have thought it a reflection upon the public to have exceeded the bounds
of probability for effect, at least of such probability
as the prescription of the stage allows: he would not
have introduced an Otaheitean° at the Lord Trea-
surer Burleigh's, nor have gone so far as to "make his
heroine blue."°

He had flattered himself into the persuasion, that
the character of Veronica was new to the stage; and,
in able hands, would produce a very laughable effect: it was written purposely for Mrs. Mattocks;°
and, if the Author is any judge of the abilities of others, Mrs. Mattocks is the only person who could have
performed it. In her line she is unrivalled; and in
her hands Veronica would have received a thousand
touches, which the pen of an author could never sup-
ply; and upon her powers the author would willingly
have risked his success.

Now, whether the piece had no merit at all, or
whether it had less merit than the dramas which have
lately been produced at Covent Garden Theatre, or
whether the Author was too obscure, and could not
fill the boxes on its appearance, certain it is, that
the piece, after a short time, was returned with a
NO; adding, that where a piece was not accepted, no
remarks or suggestions were ever made.

The Author was now thrown upon the world. As
money was his object, he did not apply to the other

winter theatre,° but presented it to the Manager of
the Haymarket Theatre; thinking it possible, if he
approved it, that he might engage Mrs. Mattocks to
perform the principal character, as he had formerly
engaged Mr. Kemble° for a similar purpose in one of
his own pieces. But Mr. Colman thought "its representation would not serve the interests of the Haymarket Theatre."

The Author had now only to reflect upon what
had been before suggested to him, that the piece was
better adapted to the closet° than the stage, as the
character of Veronica could only have its full force
with those who understood botany. This was very
true, but it was a circumstance that he was aware
of even from the beginning. He flattered himself,
that as the study of Botany was very fashionable,
and as almost every body knew something of its
outlines, the majority of an audience would understand it, and the remainder would be pleased with
the comic sound of the jargon, when delivered with
humour, though unacquainted with its literal meaning. He had heard audiences set into roars of laughter
by Lingo's bad Latin,° though perhaps four-fifths of
the audience were unacquainted with the language.
Moreover, French, Italian, German, and Scotch characters are generally received with applause, though
their language is often perfectly unintelligible.

Unwilling, like a fond parent, that his child should
remain in obscurity, the Author consigns it to the

closet,° at the same time intreating the Reader to keep in mind, that it was written principally for acting, and for the singular manner of Mrs. Mattocks, to be set off with the farther advantages of music, and the most beautiful scenery that can be imagined. Had it appeared on the stage, many parts would have been considerably curtailed, as too long for effect in representation, but which the Author hopes will, nevertheless, prove entertaining in the closet, if not absolutely essential to his design: he wished, as much as possible, to realize to his Reader the spot where he has laid his scene, that those who have seen it may recall the original to their minds, and to give the best idea of it in his power to those who have not.

It only remains to say a few words upon the objects of the ridicule. The Author assures himself he is not singular in thinking the study of Botany not altogether a proper amusement for the more polished sex; and the false taste of a licentious age, which is gaining ground, and corrupting the soft and elegant manners of the otherwise loveliest part of the creation, requires every discouragement which can be given.

SHOULD this Drama fall into any one's hands who is neither acquainted with *the Lakes*, nor *a picturesque Traveller*, nor *a Botanist*, it may be proper to recommend to his perusal, by way of

## A KEY,

West's Guide to the Lakes.°

A Journey made in the summer of 1794, through Holland and the Western Frontier of Germany, with a Return down the Rhine: to which are added, Observations during a Tour to the Lakes in Lancashire, Westmorland, and Cumberland, 4to. 1795.°

The Botanic Garden: a Poem, in Two Parts.°

Some of the Tours and Novels of the present day, &c. &c.

# PROLOGUE.

WHERE CUMBRIA'S mountains in the north arise,
Where cloud-capp'd SKIDDAW seeks the azure skies,
Nature hath shower'd from forth her lavish hand
Her choicest beauties o'er the favour'd land.
There verdant hills the fertile vales divide,
And at their base pellucid rivers glide;
Or the broad lake, outstretch'd in wide expanse,
Discovers to the trav'ler's wond'ring glance
Enchanting scenes, which captivate the soul,
And make therein delightful visions roll.
There the bleak crags their barren bosoms bare,
Stupendous cataracts hideous chasms wear,
From rock to rock they force their headlong way,
Stun with their noise, and fill the air with spray;
The hanging cliff its dreadful safety yields,
Where Jove's proud bird its annual eyrie builds.

    Thither, attracted from their peaceful home,
The Poet and the Painter love to roam,
Feed fancy full, 'till fraught with fire divine,
Their beauties on the page and canvas shine;
There CUMBERLAND° enrich'd his moral muse,

And FARRINGTON* produc'd his matchless Views.
There, too, the botanist, with prying eyes,
Culls the fair flowers in all their thousand dyes;
The teeming waters yield the scaly race,
And the keen sportsman joins the noisy chase;
Health, rosy goddess, there unharm'd resides,
And Liberty, the mountain nymph, presides.
Each season there delighted myriads throng
To pass their time these charming scenes among:
For pleasure, knowledge, many thither hie,
For fashion some, and some—they know not why.
And these same visitors, e'en one and all,
The Natives by the name of LAKERS° call.

There has our Author fix'd his Drama's Scene,
Such are his Characters, if right I ween:
A motley groupe, of various tastes, no doubt,
And each pursuing what his taste points out;
But how together brought, and what befell
These Lakers there, the Piece itself must tell.

Thus much the Prologue for the Drama says,—
And now the Author for your patience prays;
Hopes that you'll all your best of humours wear,
And to exert your candour will prepare;

* Of all the Views of the Lakes Mr. Farrington's° are perhaps
the best, and the most faithful representations; yet he has
certainly taken some liberties. Had this Prologue been written
after the opening of the Exhibition° for the present year, Mr.
W. Turner's name would have been mentioned as an artist,
whose Views of the Lakes do honour to himself and the scenes
they represent.

For I am bid to say in his behalf,
He humbly hopes that he shall make you laugh,
And, as he sows, so likewise let him reap,
And, if he makes you laugh, give not him cause to
                              [weep.

# DRAMATIS PERSONÆ.

SIR CHARLES PORTINSCALE.°
BOB KIDDY.
FIRST PEDESTRIAN.
SECOND PEDESTRIAN.
BILLY SAMPLE, *a Bagman.*°
SPEEDWELL, *Servant to* SIR CHARLES.
LANDLORD.
BEGGAR *and his Dog.*

MISS BECCABUNGA VERONICA.°
LYDIA.
ANNA KATHARINA, *their Maid.*

SCENE.—KESWICK *and its Environs.*

# THE LAKERS.

## ACT I.

### SCENE I.

*A Room at the Queen's Head.°*

*Sir Charles (without).* SPEEDWELL, see the horses taken care of; and then inquire at the Post-office whether there are any letters. (*Shown in by Landlord.*)

*Landlord.* You are welcome to Keswick again, Sir Charles.

*Sir Charles.* Thank you, Landlord.—Again and again, I hope. While Keswick displays its wonders, and health and amusement are to be acquired in surveying them, I want nothing but opportunity to bring me here oftener. Have you had much company this season? Many LAKERS?

*Landlord.* Sights of 'em, Sir. The house is now as full as it can hold; and, if any more should come in, I don't know what we shall do.

*Sir Charles.* Have you had many people of note?

*Landlord.* No, Sir. Lord Parsimony was here last week: but then you know, Sir, he travels with only a pair of horses, and orders only a pint of wine.

*Sir Charles.* A good hint, Landlord. Why you inn-keepers in the north had once the character of being civil and contented in your manners, and moderate in your charges. Now, if you retain your civility, you are certain to lose your moderation.

*Landlord.* Why, Sir, travellers used to wonder at the reasonableness of our charges, and we are not so dull as not to take a hint when it is given us.

*Sir Charles.* Yes, we must thank ourselves for that.

*Landlord.* Sir Incurious Hurry has been here too.

*Sir Charles.* He never fails. Sir Incurious is so passionately fond of travelling, and the Lakes, that he drives post through the country every year, with his carriage windows up, and never gets out but to eat, drink, and sleep.—Who else? But I must call at Crosthwaite's,° and see the list.

*Landlord.* A gentleman was here last week, who inquired after Sir Charles Portinscale. He is a Cambridge gentleman, Sir, and was here the last time you was.

*Sir Charles.* With his gun and his rod?

*Landlord.* Never a day but he was out either shooting or fishing.

*Sir Charles.* Ay, Tom Angle. The keenest sportsman that ever lived. He knows the time of every fly, from the green-drake to the palmer-fly.°

*Enter* Speedwell, *with a Letter.*

*Speed.* Only this letter, Sir.

*Sir Charles.* Very well. Landlord, I had an early dinner, so shall want some supper.—Speedwell, where are the saddle-bags? I want my pocket-book.

*Landlord.* They were carried into the bar, Sir.

[*Exit, with* Speedwell.

*Sir Charles. (Opens the letter, and reads.)*

"Dear Charles,

"Since we parted at Lancaster, I have gained some intelligence of your fair partner, which I judge adviseable to communicate to you. The aunt, whom Lydia mentioned, is Miss Beccabunga Veronica, of Diandria° Hall, a great botanist and picturesque traveller, who, with her nephew Bob Kiddy, are taking the tour of the Lakes. Miss Beccabunga has a large fortune, part of which is in her own disposal; the rest goes to Lydia, at her death. She is, I understand, very impatient for a husband——"

Yes, she has been studying the system of plants, till she now wishes to know the system of man.

——"and presuming upon Lydia's dependance upon her, during her life, insists upon having the first attack upon, and refusal of, every person who comes in their way. A title is her ambition. You must therefore fortify your heart and person against her attacks. No doubt you will see, or hear of, them again, in the course of your tour: they intend being at Keswick on the twentieth. Adieu. I wish you success. Yours, sincerely, though in haste,      H. FRIENDLY."

The twentieth! That is, to-day. Here then a new campaign opens upon me. I have to take one heart, whilst I resist the attacks of another. The service of Bellona° must, for a short time, give way to that of a milder deity.

## AIR.

*Though the Goddess of War is the mistress I serve,*
  *Yet Beauty has surely a claim;*
*From the dictates of Honour my heart will not swerve,*
  *Nor reject the bright triumph of Fame:*
*But vain is all conquest, the triumph how vain,*
  *A trifle not worth our regard,*
*Unless the dear blessing of peace to maintain,*
  *With Beauty the precious reward.*

*Enter* Speedwell, *with Saddle-bags.*

*Sir Charles.* Put down the saddle-bags, and come hither. I took you into my service, Speedwell, while you were yet very young and uninformed. Your parents, though they were poor, were honest, and by their birth deserved better then they received from the hands of fortune. Though servants, they had been faithful friends to our family; and I promised them to take care of you. That promise, I think, I have fulfilled: I have treated you more upon the footing of a friend than a servant; have taught you myself, as far as circumstances would permit, and had you instructed by others, both in your duty as a man, and in what other knowledge might be useful to you in passing away your leisure hours in innocent amusement.

*Speed.* You have never, I hope, Sir, found me wanting in gratitude for your kindness?

*Sir Charles.* By no means. I mention not these things to remind you of any obligation you may be under to me, but of the duty you owe yourself in enjoying these advantages. You have served me faithfully, and I will now put you in a way to better your prospects for life.

*Speed.* I desire no other prospect, Sir, than that of serving Sir Charles Portinscale till my death.

*Sir Charles.* You will serve me also in serving yourself. You know the whole circumstance of my meeting with a lady at the ball at Lancaster. She has my affections, and, if I can gain hers, I mean to offer her my hand. But there is an impediment in the way of our union. She has an aunt, upon whom she is dependant during her life, and who claims to herself the privilege of having the first refusal of every man they get acquainted with. I have reason to think they will be in Keswick this day, or soon. And, to screen myself from the attacks of the aunt, whilst I may have an opportunity of paying my addresses to my Lydia, I shall change characters with you. You shall introduce yourself as Sir Charles Portinscale;

and if, under that character, you should like the aunt,
and gain her consent, marry her. I will undertake to
accommodate matters after: if not, it, at any rate,
gives me an opportunity of furthering my love with
Lydia unmolested. I am not personally known to her
aunt, as she left the assembly indisposed early in the
evening. You have talents to play the part assigned
you; you know all my circumstances, and have only to
order me to attend constantly upon you, and whilst,
in surveying the prospects, you engage the aunt, I
shall find opportunities with my Lydia. I will settle
the affair with our landlord. Therefore put on your
character immediately. Get out my dressed coat from
the saddle-bags. A red coat has attractions in itself.

*Speed.* As far as concerns you, Sir, I will execute
the plot to the best of my ability. But no merce-
nary motives shall induce me to marry an undeserv-
ing woman, or one I cannot love.

*Sir Charles.*   That is a sentiment, Speedwell,
which would do honour to the heart of a peer.

[Speedwell *undoes the saddle-bags, takes out
a coloured frock with surprise, and several
brown-paper parcels, with still greater.*]

*Speed.* If the lady, Sir, is like the turkey-cock, and
flies only at the red coat, and not at the wearer, I fear
there will be no attack; for the coat has changed its
colour, and, what's more, it has changed its fashion.

*Sir Charles.* How?

*Speed. (Undoing one of the parcels.)* Pieces of

linen! I have it, Sir. If you remember, Sir, the landlady at Penrith brought a pair of saddle-bags into your room, and desired you to let a traveller be there, as the house was full; "his name was Billy Sample, from Manchester, and he was a *virry* nice young man." Now I take it, Sir, that either I through mistake, or he through design or mistake, has changed the saddle-bags, and that these are the bagman's patterns.

*Sir Charles.* How is this? the bags were padlocked.

*Speed.* Yes, Sir, but ours was a lock that opens with a spring without a key, and this is the same. I am confident that I packed them up right, for when you said that the gig was to be left behind to be repaired, and then follow us, I changed some things from the seat to the bags.

*Sir Charles.* How heedless! However, inquire for him here, and at the other house. If he is not here, you must go back to Penrith, and see after them. He may be gone another way. But, when he finds his mistake, he will be as much disappointed as I am, and perhaps come after us.

*Speed.* He's most likely coming this way, Sir; for he offered first you, and then me, *a side* in his gig.

*Sir Charles.* Well, go and inquire, and keep a look-out for the ladies. (*Exit Speedwell.*) Happy man! to have another opportunity of conversing with my Lydia, to hear her charming voice, and again be fascinated by her bewitching smile!

## AIR.

*It was not her form, nor her features so fair,*
*Her eloquent eye, nor her fine flowing hair,*
　　*Nor her wit, her good sense, nor her grace;*
*All these had their part,*
*But what captur'd my heart,*
　　*Was the smile that beam'd sweet on her face.*

*The form it may fade, and the features may change;*
*Oft wit, by its malice, true love will estrange,*
　　*And the heart from its victim will spurn;*
*But the flame I desire*
*Burns like Vesta's° pure fire,*
　　*For the smile of good-temper's eterne.*

*Enter* Speedwell.

*Speed.* Sir, I have found them both, the bagman, who has got your coat, and the lady, who has got your heart.

*Sir Charles.* What, my Lydia?

*Speed.* And her aunt, Sir. All three coming in the bagman's gig. I suppose they accepted *the side* you refused.

*Sir Charles.* Impossible!

*Speed.* It's true, as I live, Sir; and, what is more, he has got your coat on; and, still more than that, your dressed hat out of the hat-box. Here they come, Sir.

*Sir Charles.* Astonishing! let us stand aside and observe them. Take up the cloathes however.

*Enter* Veronica, Lydia, *and* Sample *in Regimentals, shown in by* Landlord, *bearing Scotch Plaid, Boxes, &c.*

*Landlord.* The party in the best room are going away immediately, and you shall have that, Madam. Here is an account of the museums. (*Gives papers.*)

*Ver.* How supremely fortunate! A guide and botanist, "well acquainted with the rare *indigenous* plants of the mountains, rocks, and lakes." I beg you'll desire the guide and botanist to repair hither directly.

*Sir Charles. (Aside to* Speed.*)* That is my cue; do you wait upon the officer. [*They retire.*]

*Ver.* Pray see all the things taken out, and bring my drawing-box instantaneously. I would not lose my sketches and the manuscript of my tour for the world. I am sure, Sir, we are under an infinitude of obligations to you for this favour. If it had not been for your kindness when the Sociable° broke down, I don't know what we could possibly have done.

*Sample.* You are very welcome, Miss. But bringing your luggage and all was rather too much. The horse is knocked up.

*Ver.* O dear, don't give yourself any uneasiness on his account. If he should die, I'll write a monody, or an epitaph, or an elegy upon him, and that will immortalize him.

*Sample.* But it won't buy me another horse.

*Ver.* But it will. Publish it on a wire-wove, hot-pressed, cream-coloured paper, with the *fac-similes* on the other side; I'll do some designs for it, and it will sell for a guinea.

*Sample.* But a guinea won't buy me a horse.

*Ver.* If it is an hundred, you shall have it. But pray, may I know to whom I am indebted for this kindness?

*Sample.* I always forget my name. It's lucky it's with-inside my hat. (*Aside, taking off his hat, and looking into it.*) Sir Charles Port-in-scale, Miss.

*Ver.* How fortunate! The elegant and accomplished Sir Charles Portinscale, and a botanist too. I must have him. (*Aside.*) To have received this favour from Sir Charles Portinscale, of whose merits the world so loudly speaks, adds weight to the obligation, and makes it inestimable.

*Sample.* And pray, Miss, what's your name?

*Ver.* You do me infinite honour, Sir Charles; my name is Beccabunga Veronica, of Diandria Hall; my *hybernaculum*° is in Grosvenor Square.——Lydia—

*Sample.* Well, Miss Becky Bungay——

*Ver.* Why, Lydia, why don't you acknowledge Sir Charles? You know you danced with him at Lancaster.

*Lydia.* I had the honour of dancing with Sir Charles Portinscale at Lancaster. But it was not for me to speak first. What can this mean? (*Aside.*)

*Ver.* Sir Charles, you don't seem to recollect your partner?

*Sample.* My partner!

*Ver.* Don't you remember at Lancaster assize-ball? I unfortunately danced the two first dances in a different set, and was then taken so ill as to be obliged to go home.

*Sample.* I wasn't at——Plague on't! I forget who I am. (*Aside.*) O ay; we danced Morgan Ratler.°

*Enter* Speedwell.

*Speed.* I have seen the horses taken care of, Sir, ordered your bed, and a bird and bottle for supper.

*Sample.* Taken care of!—bird and bottle!

*Speed.* I got here just half an hour before you, Sir.

*Ver.* Is this your servant, Sir Charles?

*Speed.* I have the honour, Madam, to serve Sir Charles Portinscale.

*Ver.* You never told us of him, Sir Charles. I did not know you had a servant with you.

*Sample.* Nor I neither. (*Aside.*)

*Ver.* It was very unlucky he was gone on when our *voiture*° broke down, or he might have assisted us in our *pericula.*°

*Sample.* That's the name of your carriage, is it? You called it a Sociable just now. He might have brought one of you behind him.

*Ver.* Ride double! how unpicturesque! If you have no objection, Sir Charles, we will join parties, and add something to your roast fowl and bottle.

*Sample.* Roast fowl and bottle! 'twould eat up all my profits. I shall only have a bit of cold meat and sixpen'orth of brandy and water.

*Enter* Sir Charles, *in* Sample's *Cloathes.*

*Sir Charles.* Oh! the ladies who want me are in this room. (*Without.*) Does your Ladyship want me? I am the guide and botanist, Ma'am.——I am the guide and botanist, Ma'am. (*Significantly to Lydia.*) Sir Charles Portinscale, I am the guide and botanist. (*To Sample.*)

*Lydia.* What, my partner at Lancaster! Was he an impostor then, or is he now? My heart tells me he is true, and I am willing to be guided by him.

*Sample.* Why, what can this mean? This must be Sir Charles, and in my cloathes. Well, if he won't know me, I'm sure I don't wish to know him; and, if he likes my cloathes better than his own, he shall have 'em. I shall sooner make a fortune by a red coat, than by riding for Dimity and Co.° (*Aside.*)

*Ver.* (*Looking through glasses.*) A vastly picturesque figure, I declare! Extremely interesting!

What, you are the *Ciceroni*° of Derwent-water? I see, Mr. Botanist, that you have complete collections of the plants of the country, ready packed to send off. I desire I may have a collection.

*Sir Charles.* If your Ladyship will give me your direction, you may depend upon their being sent.

*Ver.* I must have them now. I desire you'll get them directly.

*Sir Charles.* I fear I have not a complete collection by me.

*Speed. (Aside.)* Suppose, Sir, you give her one of the bagman's parcels. She will not undo it before she goes away from hence.

*Sir Charles.* I believe here is a collection I was just going to direct and send off; but your Ladyship shall have them.

*Ver.* Very obliging, indeed! What do they come to? What is the appretiation of them?

*Sir Charles.* A guinea, if you please, Madam.

*Ver.* Sir Charles, may I beg the favour of you to pay for them? Pray untie and let me inspect them.

*Sir Charles.* I beg they may not be undone before you get home, as it would expose them to the air, and they might suffer from it. Your Ladyship shall see another parcel undone before you leave Keswick.

*Ver.* Vastly well. Sir Charles, I beg the favour of a guinea?

*Sample.* I think, Miss Becky, you had better expose them. Why, you wouldn't give a guinea for a parcel of patterns?

*Ver.* Patterns! We call them specimens, Sir Charles.

*Sample.* Sp*ice*men! Why she doesn't think she's buying a bale of gingerbread nuts. But I forget myself. (*Aside—gives a guinea.*) There, Sir, if they are not right, you give the guinea back again.—— It's very hard to give a guinea for my own goods, when they're not worth it, and not have 'em neither. If he doesn't pay me, I'll melt the gold lace off his coat and pay myself. (*Aside.*)

*Ver.* I dare say they are all right. There are the *lichens* amongst them, I hope?

*Sample.* Yes, she's a *liking* for my guinea, I see. (*Aside.*)

*Ver.* Sir Charles, I shall rest your debtor.

*Sample.* I hope not, Miss.

*Ver.* I shall beg, Mr. Botanist, to deposit my bust and leg in your museum.

*Sir Charles.* Your Ladyship will do me infinite honour, even by setting your foot in it.

*Ver.* Very prettily turned indeed.

*Sample.* Your leg, Miss?

*Ver.* I am a bit of a sculptor, and model in plaster. I had finished one exquisite bust of myself, so classical, but I spoiled it in the baking. I have, however, succeeded tolerably well in my second attempt: but every body says my leg is the finest they ever saw, and it is now in the possession of every lover of *vertu.*°

*Sample.* Well, Miss Becky, I don't see much virtue in it, but I should like to see your legs; though I always thought ladies wished to hide 'em.

*Ver.* O dear, no! quite the contrary. I played a breeches-part at my theatricals purposely to show my leg. I have just perfected a highly finished colossal statue of the Polish dwarf° in marble: I hewed it even from the block, and presented it to Lord Tasteless, and he has entirely spoiled it by putting brass buckles, sword-hilt, and lace to the hat.

*Sample.* Why, 'twould ha'been handsomer if he'd gone to the expense of silver.

*Ver.* We had better take a short perambulation before supper.

*Sir Charles.* If your Ladyship pleases. An evening prospect from Crow Park° is reckoned particularly fine. And, if we go now, we shall have the advantage of both the sunset and the rising moon.

*Lydia.* I beg, Madam, that we may go. I am cramped with sitting in the carriage, and make no doubt I shall be better for the walk.

*Ver.* I would not lose it for the world. What a fine description it will make in my tour. Sir Charles, what say you to a turn? You must take infinite pleasure in viewing the delightful and impressive scenes of this country, as you travel through it?

*Sample.* Why, Miss, I used to stare about me a good deal, when I first came, from the novelty of the thing. But, now I'm used to it, I think no more of 'em than nothing at all: I think of nothing but taking orders.

*Ver.* Bless me, Sir Charles, I hope you don't think of leaving the army?

*Sample.* Leaving the army, Miss!—O ay—O no, Miss.

*Ver.* You talked of going into the church.

*Sample.* The church!

*Ver.* You said you thought of nothing but *taking orders.*

*Sample.* O yes, Miss, for our house. I get my living by it.

*Ver.* What, you've a family living?

*Sample.* I've no family, Miss, but I don't care how soon I have one.

*Ver.* O Sir Charles, you might leave that for your second son—particularly if your wife has a fortune.

*Sample.* I should not at all mind giving up my travelling business to my son.

*Ver.* By no means, Sir Charles; I am a traveller myself.

*Sample.* Are you, Miss? What house do you travel for? Where are your patterns?

*Ver.* You will call them patterns, Sir Charles— Specimens.

*Sample.* Sp*ice*men! What, you travel for one of the great West India merchants?

*Ver.* I hope to travel for all the world.

*Sample.* That's too much to hope, Miss.

*Ver.* Not at all, I hope——I mean to make a thousand pounds by my tour.

*Sample.* That's doing business well. But I don't wonder at it. I am sure I could not refuse giving an order to such a nice creature. But I never heard of a woman traveller before.

*Ver.* Bless me, Sir Charles, why they're quite common.

*Sample.* Well, if I was married, my wife should go one way and I another.

*Ver.* That is the modern fashion to be sure: but I cannot say I should like it.

*Sample.* Why then we'd go together. I'd travel in the Manchester line, and you in the West India.

*Ver.* Why, that would be travelling the same way with a witness.°

*Sample.* Yes, yes, we should witness each other's dealings.

*Ver.* A vastly singular man is this Sir Charles. Not very polished, nor very accomplished. However, I must have him. His fortune and title are both good, and I shall have the merit of improving him. (*Aside.*) Pray, Sir Charles, could you be contented to be a *monogynia*\* all your life?

*Sample.* Be contented to bemoan my guinea here all my life! (*Half aside.*) No, Miss, I can't say I

---

\* *Monogynia*, in botanic language, signifies possessing one female.

should.

*Ver.* O fie, Sir Charles! I know you captains are great rovers, but you should not own it. Well then, a *digynia*?

*Sample.* Die for my guinea here! (*Half aside.*) No, not that neither, Miss.

*Ver.* Horrid! What must you be—a *trigynia*, or a *tetragynia*, or a *pentagynia*\*?

*Sample.* Yes, (*Half aside.*) I've spent my guinea here.

*Ver.* An absolute Turk! I wonder you should say so on my account. Why, you would not keep a seraglio?

*Sample.* If it is not on your account, I don't know on whose it is.——I don't understand three words she says. I never heard such lingo before. (*Aside.*) Well, Miss, suppose we walk.

*Ver.* If you please, Sir Charles, I shall beg the favour of your arm. Here, Mr.———what is your name?

*Speed.* Speedwell, at your service, Madam.

*Ver.* A vastly good name, indeed.—Pray take my glasses and my drawing-book, and my fishing-stool. Come, Lydia; why, you look as strange——Come, I wish you'd study botany. Do, Mr. Botanist, instruct her a little; show her a *cryptogamy*† or two.

*Sample.* What game's that, Miss?

---

\* Having five females.    † Clandestine marriage.

*Sir Charles.* I'll show her one your Ladyship never saw.

*Ver.* Oh no, I protest against it. I must have the first sight of it myself. Is it an *ophioglossum*, a *jungermania*, a *lycoperdon*, or a *polypodium*?°

*Sir Charles.* I think it will prove one of the *filices* (vice *felices**).°

*Ver.* I must see it. Come, let us be walking.— Where is my *parasol*?

*Sir Charles.* You will scarce have any use for it, Madam.

*Ver.* O yes, it will give me a more picturesque effect.

*Lydia (as they go out).* Sir Charles, this must be explained.

*Sir Charles.* Be assured it shall, and to your satisfaction. [*Exeunt.*

---

* Or an happy one.

## SCENE II.

*The Market-Place.*

*A Beggar and his Dog—The Dog sitting upon his hind Legs.*

## SONG.

### Beggar.

*Oppress'd with grief, depriv'd of sight,*
*My cheerful day is turn'd to night,*
　　*For all is dark to me;*
*No house to shelter o'er my head,*
*And forc'd to beg my daily bread:*
　　*Pray bestow your charity.*

*Your battles I have fought abroad,*
*Whilst you were at your festive board,*
　　*And all was mirth and glee;*
*Then, cold and hunger'd, have I lain*
*Upon the damp and desert plain:*
　　*Pray bestow your charity.*

*A trifle now is all I crave*
*To rescue from the gaping grave*
　　*My faithful dog and me.*
*O give—and for the friendly boon,*
*Just Heav'n shall shower its mercies down:*
　　*Pray bestow your charity.*

*At the end of the first verse* Veronica *enters, leaning on* Sample*'s arm;* Lydia *talking with* Sir Charles; *and* Speedwell *following.* Veronica *listens attentively, gives her parasol to* Sample *to hold, and stands in an attitude. After the second verse, she exclaims,* "How interesting!" *After the third,* "And the little dog too! Dear creature! What a powerful appeal to a too susceptible heart! How happy should I be to do any thing for the amelioration of his condition!—Sir Charles, have you got any halfpence?"

*Sample.* What, more money! She'll brozier° me. (*Aside.*) No, Miss, I have not.

*Ver.* Then a sixpence?

*Sample.* Not a sixpence, Miss.

*Ver.* Then a shilling, I beg. I saw one when you took out your purse just now.

*Sample.* I don't like her tricks upon travellers. But as I'm a great man, and her lovier, I suppose she must have it. (*Aside.*) There, Miss, that makes one pound two.

*Ver.* Don't disturb these amiable feelings of refined sensibility. (*Drops the shilling into the beggar's hat—pauses—takes out her handkerchief, and puts it to her eyes.*)

*Beggar.* Heaven bless you!

*Sample.* You need not cry, Miss; the loss is mine, and not yours.

*Ver.* Lead me away. These quick vibrations of the

fine fibres of my heart are too much for so slender a frame.

*Sample.* Well, but you see I don't cry.

*Ver.* Stop, Sir Charles. I shall lose the force of it, if I don't write it down while the impression is warm. (*Takes out her book, and writes.*)

*Speed.* This may be feeling and charity, but I can't exactly tell.

## SONG.

> *If, when the poor ask charity,*
> *Without a thought you pass them by,*
> *And answer not their claim;*
> *Whate'er excuse*
> *You may produce,*
> *It is a burning shame.*

> *But when, to gratify your pride,*
> *At their request you turn aside,*
> *And in their sorrows pry;*
> *Why then in truth,*
> *'Tis little worth,*
> *Your charity is all my eye.*

> *And if by chance you freely give,*
> *Accordingly as you receive,*
> *And as they urge their claim,*
> *And then should cry*
> *And wipe your eye,*
> *It is a crying shame.*

*Ver.* I think I have succeeded in my *Notitium.*°
(*Reads from her book.*) "As we were crossing the
market-place, in our way from the *auberge*° to Crow
Park, my ears were struck with some of the most interesting sounds I ever heard, and which irresistibly
arrested my footsteps. It was a blind beggar, relat-
ing in plaintive numbers his melancholy story. By
his side he had a dumb, but an able advocate, who,
with mute eloquence, made the most forcible appeal
to one's charity. A little dog was attached to his
side, who, in a supplicatory posture, joined in the
eleemosynary° claims of his master. I dropped a trifle into the maimed mendicant's hat with a tear—
—another was about to follow it, but, ashamed of
the amiable weakness, I caught the foolish pearl in
my handkerchief, and treasured it up in the faithful
repository of my bosom." There, I think that a very
*happy* sentence. What is your opinion, Sir Charles?

*Sample.* I think it a *miserable* one, Miss.

*Ver.* I don't know how I could alter it for the better, unless I were to put "napkin" instead of "handkerchief," for the sake of *euphony.*

*Sample.* For whose sake, Miss? You may call it
"muckinder," if you like it better.

*Ver.* I really believe he has a mind to laugh at
me. I may perhaps introduce a quotation or two.
Perhaps, Sir Charles, you can give me a line or two
from Horace, or Juvenal, or Tacitus, or———; but
that will do when I come to make it out fuller. I think

it is perspicuously enarrated. Come, Mr. Botanist, pray show us the way: the day is getting deciduous.°
Farewell, my friend; I sympathize in the secret of your sorrows. (*Sir Charles and Lydia give him money.*)

*Speed.* I can neither sport with his feelings nor my own. (*Gives money.*)          [*Exeunt.*

## AIR.

### Beggar.

*Be gracious, Heaven! and give reward*
*To all who thus the poor regard,*
*And grant that they may never know*
*The beggar's piercing wants and woe!*

## SCENE III.

### *Crow Park.*

*The scene represents the view cross* Derwent-water *into the gorge of* Borrowdale, *and* Lowdore *water-fall in the distance. The front of the stage represents* Crow Park; *about the middle, towards the right hand side, is* Vicar's Island, *with the house seen sideways, the church in full view. The warm glow of sunset pervades the landscape at first, and gradually dies away. A short interval of gloom succeeds, and the moon then rises from behind the mountains of* Borrowdale.

Veronica *enters with a bunch of flowers in her hand,* Sir Charles *on one side of her and* Sample *on the other,* Lydia *following, and* Speedwell *at a distance, carrying* Veronica*'s paraphernalia.*

*Ver.* A vastly curious plant indeed, Mr. Botanist! A *non-descript,*° you say?

*Sample.* You gather herbs, do you? What, are you any thing of a doctor?

*Ver.* It's a *tetrandria tetragynia,* I see. The *peduncle* is *articulated, membranaceous, umbelliferous,* and *tomentose*; as are also the *petioles.* The leaves are *cauline, petioled,* and *lanceolate*; the *corolla* is *polypetalous*; the *calyx* is *monophyllous*; the *pericarpium* is *tricoccous*; and the *semen* a *nux.*° We must give it a name, Mr. Botanist. Wait a short time, and we will call it, from myself, the Portinscalia. (*Aside to him.*)

*Sir Charles.* It will be a long time, if we wait till then. (*Aside.*)

*Sample. (Aside).* What a deal to have to say to one little bit of a plant! Poor woman! I am afraid she does not know what she's talking about.

*Ver.* I must have a specimen for my *hortus siccus.*° Sir Charles, you don't seem to admire it.

*Sample.* I don't think much of it indeed, Miss. The colour's so dim, and it's got no smell.

*Ver.* Why, what botanist ever thought of colour or smell in a plant? Speedwell, give me my botany box. (*Puts plants in.*) There, take care of it.

*Sample.* What, I suppose you press 'em in books? I've seen a many do so. But I never could think what they were for, unless it was for making patterns for printing cotton.

*Ver.* O Sir Charles! I am no stranger to your perfect knowledge of the Linnæan system.

*Sample.* I think, Miss, I do know a good deal about linens.

*Ver.* Intensely astonishing! Pray, Sir Charles; do you understand German?

*Sample.* No, Miss——not your jargon. (*Aside.*)

*Ver.* Why every body of taste reads German now. I design to work up the story of the Visionary Horseman on Souther-Fell-side° into a ballad in imitation of the German.

*Sir Charles.* This, Madam, is the celebrated lake of Keswick, or Derwent-water; and the place where we now are, Crow Park, Mr. West's second station. It was formerly a glade of ancient oaks, but the wasting hand of avarice has spoiled it of its beauties.

*Ver.* Oh! if one single tree had remained, this would have been an unparalleled spot! Stop a minute, if you please, Mr. *Ciceroni*, while I get out my pencil to write. (*She writes while he gives his account.*)

*Sir Charles.* This spacious amphitheatre of picturesque mountains, with the pellucid waters lying at their base, variegated with islands, adorned with wood, or clothed with the sweetest verdure, presents a picture as fine as the imagination can form. You look directly across the lake, for three miles, into the gorge of Borrowdale, where Castle Crag guards the tremendous pass. To the left is the renowned cataract of Lowdore, now seen only as a silvery streak on the side of the mountains. Ashness Crag towers to its left, and Falcon Crag, Wallow Crag, and Castle Hill, are the mountains which sweep beyond them. The fine range of fells to the right (for every crag of every mountain has its name), are Grange-fells, Goldscope, Catbells, Newlands, High-style, Red-pike, and Cawsey-pike; Barrow and Swinside below it, with the thick woods of Foe-park at their feet.

This lake is often troubled with what are called "bottom winds:" being a commotion of the water, as if agitated by a sudden gust, without any real hurricane or apparent cause.

The island nearest to us is Vicar's Island; beyond, to the left, Lord's Island, once the property of the unfortunate family of Radcliffs Earls of Derwent-water; beyond that, Rampsholm; and to the right, beyond Vicar's, is St. Herbert's Island, where he had a hermitage, the foundations of which are now visible.

*Ver.* A very happy thought, I declare: quite a *beau idée!*° You must know, Sir Charles, I have always several works in hand at the same time; and, as I always introduce a great deal of description of scenery in my romances, I keep that in my eye while I am travelling, and write a romance at the same time with my tour. It is only putting Geneva for Windermere, and, though I have never been abroad, I describe the scenery exactly as well as if I had been there. But I think I shall lay the scene of my next upon Derwent-water, make St. Herbert to have murdered a pilgrim, who shall turn out to be his brother, and I shall call it "The Horrors of the Hermitage." I can introduce a mysterious monk of Borrowdale, and shall have fine opportunities of describing luxuriant groves and bowery lanes, in all the pomp of foliage of beech, birch, mountain-ash, and holly. It shall be a romance of the fourteenth century; the castle upon Lord's Island shall be haunted by an armed head: and, I believe, Lydia, I shall draw my heroine from either you or myself, and make her passionately fond of drawing and botany; she shall be mistress of the Linnæan system*, and then, if I should make her stop, in the midst of her distresses, to admire the scenery, or gather a plant, it will be perfectly natural.

*Sample.* What a villain! murder his brother! Why he didn't murder his brother, did he?

*Ver.* Not that I know of.

*Sample.* Why, you wouldn't go to tell lies about the dead then, would you? If his relations were to

---

* Linnæus lived in the present century.

take it up, they might put you into the pillory for a libel.

*Ver.* Sir Charles!——But I will not be insulted by him. I will not suffer him to break it off. (*Aside.*)— —Vastly impressive scenery indeed; and quite accordant with my solemn tone of feeling at this moment. Pray where is Saddleback?

*Sir Charles.* Behind you, Madam, beyond Skiddaw, where the sun is now setting.

*Sample.* She carries her saddle-bags behind her too when she travels. She's a rum one, as ever I met with.

*Ver.* How infinitely sublime! Is not it, Sir Charles?

*Sample.* Yes, Miss, it's very mountainious. You are in the mountain-scenery line, I see.

*Ver.* Speedwell, give me my glasses. Where's my Gray? (*Speedwell gives glasses.*) Oh! Claude and Poussin are nothing. By the bye, where's my Claude-Lorrain? I must throw a Gilpin tint over these magic scenes of beauty. (*Looks through the glass.*) How gorgeously glowing! Now for the darker. (*Looks through the glass.*) How gloomily glaring! Now the blue. (*Pretends to shiver with cold.*) How frigidly frozen! What illusions of vision! The effect is inexpressibly interesting. The amphitheatrical perspective of the long landscape; the peeping points of the many-coloured crags of the headlong mountains, looking out most interestingly from the picturesque luxuri-

ance of the bowery foliage, margining their rugged-
ness, and feathering the fells; the delightful differences of the heterogeneous masses; the horrific mountains, such scenes of ruin and privation! the turfy
hillocks, the umbrageous° and reposing hue of the
copsy lawns, so touchingly beautiful; the limpid lapse
of Lowdore, the islands coroneting the flood; the water, the soft purple of the pigeon's neck,—are so many
circumstances of imagery, which all together combine
a picture, which for its sentimental beauty and assem-
blages of sublimity, I never exceeded in the warmest
glow of my fancied descriptions.   And then the in-
comparable verdure of the turfy slope we are upon;
the water bickering at the base; the sultry low of the
cattle, sipping the clear wave, add a sweet pathos to
the magical effect of the surrounding scenery.   And
now the effulgence of the sunshine landscape is fad-
ing away, and the blue distances, stealing upon the
nearer view, soften the sublime severity.—I must take
a sketch.——Sir Charles, pray come and stand by me
for the trunk of an old tree in the foreground.   And I
beg, Mr. Botanist, you and Lydia and Speedwell will
form yourselves into a picturesque group.

*Sample.*   What, Miss, you° are a planner, I see;
and are come to look about you and spy your fancies.
Pray, Miss, what's this you call your Cordovan?

*Ver.*   My Claude-Lorrain! It is a *deceptio visus*,°
an artifice to give the various tints of the changes of
weather and season to the landscape.

*Sample (looking through).* Well, Miss, if that's your fancy, I should think it would be less trouble always to wear a pair of green or yellow spectacles.

*Ver.* Where's my fishing-stool? (*Sits down.*) Your arm up, if you please, Sir Charles, for the branch of the tree. Mr. Botanist, pray mind the group. Suppose you sing, Mr. Botanist? Lydia, you, and perhaps Speedwell, can make up a glee. It will, at least, give picturesqueness to my description.

*Sir Charles.* If the lady will honour us in joining.

## GLEE.

*From forth her interlunar cave*
*The silver moon has tipp'd the wave,*
*And from the distant rocky shore*
*The falling water's sullen roar,*
*Borne on the gently swelling gale,*
*Fraught with the sweets o'th' flow'ry vale,*
*Steal on the watchful ear of night,*
*Diffuse a solemn still delight,*
*Which to tir'd nature, her sweet guest,*
*Imparting, lulls her to her rest.*

*Ver. Bravi! Bravissimi! mio botanist carissimo!*° You have given energy to my humble talents; your poetry and music have given life to their sister art, and I feel myself peculiarly happy in my little sketch. Pray look at it, Sir Charles, and give me your opinion.

*Sample.* Why, it's no more like the thing than——
Why, you've made the hills more like sugar-loaves—

*Ver.* If it is not like what it *is*, it is what it *ought*
to be. I have only made it picturesque.

*Sir Charles.* The painter has always a licence to
improve upon Nature, where she has erred or been
deficient.

*Ver.* Certainly. I have only given the hills an
Alpine form, and put some wood where it is wanted,
and omitted it where it is not wanted: and who could
put that sham church and that house into a picture?
It quite *antipathizes.* I don't like such meretricious
ornaments.

*Sample.* Why, that place is a tea-garden, I suppose.

*Ver.* Ha! ha! you are vastly witty, Sir Charles.
Not a bad comparison of yours.

*Sir Charles.* Your Ladyship forgets the motto to
the island: *"De gustibus non est disputandum."*°

*Ver.* Gustibus!—disput!—Pray, Sir Charles, what
does that mean?

*Sample.* What can I say? (*Aside.*) Oh, aye!—"It
is not to be disputed but there are gusts upon the
lake."

*Ver.* Oh! alluding to the bottom winds, I suppose.
But what has that to do, Mr. Botanist, with——?
Well—so, I have made the church an old abbey, the
house a castle, and the battery an hermitage: I have
broken the smooth surface of the water with water-

lilies, flags,° flowering rushes, water-docks, and other aquatics, making it more of a plashy inundation than a basin of water: then I have put in for the foreground the single tree they ought to have left standing, an ancient tree of remarkable size and venerable beauty; and have sprinkled some ferns, and burdocks, and gorse, and thistles, over this turfy slope. I must, I think, do this in colours: an orange sky, yellow water, a blue bank, a green castle, and brown trees, will give it a very fine effect. Sir Charles, how do you like it?

*Sample.* I can't make neither head nor tail on't. Why, Miss, you might as well draw a head with a goggle eye and a hooked nose, a wide mouth and a double chin, and give it a beard and a wig, and call it my picture.

*Ver.* Sir Charles!—(*A flute is heard at a distance playing the air of "A Shepherd once."*° Veronica *drops her book and her pencil, and stands listening.*) What a picturesque sound! The very tune too of my own little *ariette.* A fine opportunity for displaying my vocal powers. (*Aside.*)

## ARIETTE.

*A lady once her lap-dog lost, Bow, wow, wow, &c.*
*And she knew it to her cost; Bow, wow, wow, &c.*
*For all in vain the search was tried, Bow, wow, &c.*
*Until his mistress had him cried. Bow, wow, &c.*

*When at last was Pompey found, Bow, wow, &c.*
*All the house with grief did sound;*
*For, oh! some cruel-hearted wight*
*A piece of sponge had made him eat.*

*This at length, in hour accurst, Bow, wow, &c.*
*Swell'd till it did make him burst;*
*His mistress felt with him the smart,*
*And for him she did break her heart.*

*Sample.* Well, that's a pretty song, Miss Becky.

*Ver.* You do me infinite honour, Sir Charles: but I am not altogether in voice this evening.—He's not so ignorant and tasteless as I imagined; but he's an unaccountable man: he's a humourist, I believe. (*Aside.*)

*Sir Charles.* Does your Ladyship observe a party in a boat making fast to the shore?

*Ver.* And the dashing of the oars breaking the solemn silence of the evening. Vastly fine, indeed. They are going to land here, I declare. How it heightens the interest of the scene!

(*A boat makes to the shore of Crow Park. The company in it sing,* Veronica *and her party join the chorus.*)

## AIR *and* CHORUS.

*With equal stroke, the dashing oar*
*Gains upon the moonlight shore,*
*And, with day's busy cares opprest,*
*Releases us to joy and rest.*

END OF THE FIRST ACT.

# ACT II.

## SCENE I.

*A Room at the Queen's Head.*

*Enter* Sir Charles *and* Speedwell.

*Sir Charles.*

IF we go on in this manner, Speedwell, it is impossible but our schemes must fail. That ignorant booby, Sample, has no more idea of personating the character he has assumed, than—

*Speed.* A cow has of dancing a hornpipe, Sir.

*Sir Charles.* About as much. How unlike he is to many of his profession! I have conversed with some who have been men of good sense and considerable information; but he seems to think, that it is only putting on the dress, and he becomes the character without farther trouble. If Veronica were not blinded by vanity, folly, and botanic nuptials, she must have immediately discovered the imposition.

*Speed.* Well, Sir, it is but having recourse, at last, to your original plan. Suppose we confess the imposture, say I am the real Sir Charles Portinscale, who assumed the disguise of a servant to contemplate her charms unobserved himself, and that Sample is my servant? You, Sir, may still retain your character of guide and botanist.

*Sir Charles.* Not a bad scheme, Speedwell: but how shall we get Sample to come into it?

*Speed.* Why, Sir, there is an argument that I have often known to be made use of, and which is sure of prevailing when all others fail—the *argumentum baculinum.°* You have acquiesced in his imposture so long as it was practicable; and, if he will not come into yours, no doubt the rattan will convince him of the necessity of it.

*Sir Charles.* But the fellow has not talents to personate even a servant well. Take him from his profits and his patterns, and he has not three ideas beyond.

*Speed.* If he is awkward, Sir, it is only sending him to the stable or the kitchen.

*Sir Charles.* Of your talents I have no doubt: you so well know my circumstances, my manners, and even my acquirements, from copying over my writings, from books I have recommended to you, and from our conversation on the road, that I question whether your knowledge does not exceed Veronica's. I have often explained to you the outlines of Linnæus's System of Vegetables; you therefore can very well

*In filmy, gawsy, gossamery lines,°*
*With lucid language and conceal'd designs,*
*In sweet monandrian monogynian° strains*
*Pant for your mistress in botanic pains.*

*Speed.* Bating the hard words, Sir, I think I can match Veronica from the marriage of one male and one female to the clandestine marriages of Gretna Green. I thought, as soon as I saw Sample, that it might come to this, and therefore was not idle with my eyes. I think, Sir, some glances, which I cast upon her, were not thrown away. Here comes the adventurous knight, Sir: we will dispel the enchantment which holds him.

*Enter* Sample.

*Sample.* Here they are both together. I don't know what to say. (*Aside.*) Go, Speedwell, and see the horses taken care of.——Why don't you go?

*Speed.* I am no servant of yours, Sir.

*Sample.* Why, you said yourself you was.

*Speed.* When you said you were Sir Charles Portinscale.

*Sample.* I hav'n't said I'm not he.

*Speed.* But we do, Sir. Here is the true Sir Charles, and you are only an impostor.

*Sample.* I think he's an impostor.

*Sir Charles.* Come, Sir, I will explain matters. By mistake we exchanged luggage; you got my regimentals, and I your frock and patterns. Deprived of your business by the loss, I suppose you wished to indemnify yourself, by making your fortune with the red coat. You appeared to be making up to the lady I wished to avoid, and I therefore acquiesced in your scheme till you ruined it yourself. You have disgusted the lady; and, unless the imposture is confessed, she must discover it herself.

*Speed.* That is, Sir, you have put on the lion's skin; but the long ears, and your braying, have betrayed you.°

*Sir Charles.* In short, Sir, it is impossible for you to succeed with her; and, as I have an interest to serve, you must come into my schemes, in return for my acquiescence in yours. My affections are fixed upon the niece, and, were I to declare myself, I should lose her, and expose myself to the attacks of the aunt. My farther disguise is therefore necessary, and, to countenance that, my servant must declare you an impostor, that he is the true Sir Charles, and you must consent to pass for his servant.

*Sample.* No, don't you think it. I won't demean myself to be servant to a servant. You yourself said I was Sir Charles, and you can't confess having told a lie.

*Sir Charles.* Then this, Sir, is the alternative. The imposture must be acknowledged, and you must relinquish your character. Our luggage must be re-exchanged; I have my regimentals, and you your frock and patterns; for that mistake, we can only be sorry for the inconvenience it has occasioned. But, Sir, recollect my *hat* was left in the care of the landlord, and by what felonious means you became possessed of it, I know not; that you must explain to the justice, before whom you will be taken to give an account.

*Speed.* I beg, Sir, that may be deferred a short time. I have received an insult from him; he said "he would not *demean* himself to be servant to a servant," meaning me; and I beg that I may first have an opportunity of satisfying my honour, by calling him out to fight me with pistols, or, if he refuses me that satisfaction, I may kick him through Keswick.

*Sample.* Justice! Pistols! Kicked through Keswick! Well, but now if I consent?

*Sir Charles.* I shall be satisfied.

*Speed.* And so will my honour. It will be a recantation.

*Sample.* And I shall have my patterns back, and you'll pay me my guinea?

*Sir Charles.* And satisfy you for any other loss you may have been at.

*Speed.* And give him an order, Sir, for a piece of cloth, to make waistcoats.

*Sample.* It's a bargain then; and I shall be glad to get into my own cloathes again; for I feel a little awkward in these. It's harder to be a baronet and a captain than I thought for: I find it is not the scarlet coat and gold lace that makes the officer.

*Sir Charles.* Come, then, Speedwell, you and Mr. Sample must change cloathes, and the sooner the discovery is made the better.

*Speed.* I shall be changed in an instant, Sir.

## SONG.

*The cameleon, it's true,*
*Changes scarlet, green, or blue,*
*    As the ground that by chance it shall rest on:*
*In my master's livery*
*His humble slave am I;*
*If dress'd at my own charge,*
*I'm the gentleman at large,*
*    And my master's own self with his best on.*

Sample.

*Well pleas'd, now I've tried,*
*I'm to lay my rank aside,*
*    And to put off the clothes that I've stept in;*
*None e'er, that I could hear,*
*Could make purse of a pig's ear;*
*Nor can waistcoat and coat*
*Make the gentleman, I wot;*
*    Nor the hat and cockade make the captain.*
                    [*Exit with* Speedwell.

### Sir Charles.

*Wheree'er we turn our eyes,*
*The world is all disguise,*
*From the first to the last 'tis deception:*
*The gentleman lets down,*
*Dress'd and manner'd as a clown;*
*The clown his betters apes,*
*His dress and manner shapes,*
*And appears of the better description.*

*Enter* Veronica, *her hair partly done up in a silk net,*
*partly hanging loose, a straw hat and green veil,*
*her gown fantastically drawn up.*

*Ver.* Mr. Botanist, I am infinitely distressed, quite in despair, that we cannot go up Skiddaw this morning.

*Sir Charles.* Skiddaw has got his nightcap on, Madam, and, were we to go up, we could not see any thing of the surrounding country.

*Ver.* Well, I'll wait till to-morrow morning, and then I must go up whether it is fine or not. My tour would be absolutely incomplete without an account of a ride up Skiddaw. I can assure you I had dressed on purpose for the expedition.

*Sir Charles.* You would have found that dress rather too light and airy for that cold atmosphere.

*Ver.* Not at all. You must have taken my Scotch plaid to have thrown round me when the air became very thin. A riding-habit would not have done at all in that mountain region; it would have broken in upon the *costumé.*° So I have negligently bound up my hair in a silk net, and suffered some tresses to escape to play upon my neck and round my countenance. And then the light drapery of my dress, my straw hat, the veil partially concealing my face, my figure and my air, are what might, I think, be copied for a Grecian nymph.

*Sir Charles. (Aside.)* A Grecian nymph in a Scotch plaid, upon the mountains of Cumberland! What a preservation of the *costume*!

*Ver.* However, it will equally accord with the scenery round Derwent-water: I shall appear like the Naïad of Lowdore, or the nymph of Borrowdale.

*Sir Charles.* Your Ladyship is very considerate. Were an artist to be there at the same time, he must think himself singularly happy in having so charming a figure to give life to his landscape.

*Ver.* You are vastly obliging, Mr. Botanist. I have sat once to Mr. Daubly° for my picture, which is to be finished against the next exhibition. I am depicted as the modern goddess of botany: I am sitting upon the stump of a tree, which has been grafted with innumerable different kinds of shrubs—the various *Syringas*: *foliis ovato-cordatis, foliis lanceolatis*; the *Cytisas*, the *Cestras*, the *Lycias*, *Loniceras*;°—which branch round and form a bower over my head. Every flower springs up around me, and a water-fall dashes by my side: I have a full-blown moss-rose upon my

head instead of a cap, and moss-rose buds hanging
about my neck and shoulders, instead of hair. Two
wreaths of honeysuckle twine round my neck and my
waist, and under my garment, which is slightly drawn
up, instead of a stocking, appears the bark of a tree.

*Sir Charles. (Aside.)* The goddess of botany with
a wooden leg!

*Ver.* My feet are covered with the *conferva rivularis*,° with a large rose upon each of them. In my
hand I hold my poem, in twenty cantos, "The Triumph of Botany," while the Arts and Sciences are all
paying homage to me. The *coup d'œil*° is exceedingly
fine; and I do not recollect to have seen any thing like
it before.

*Sir Charles.* Not exactly, Madam——except the
owl in the ivy-bush.° (*Aside.*)

*Ver.* I mentioned my poem: the subject is, I
think, extremely interesting, and purely classical.
You know, Sir, that the botanist and the florist have
long been at variance; the florist only esteems a
few, and those chiefly the double flowers, which the
botanist considers as monsters. Now I suppose, that,
after repeated hostilities, which are the subject of the
former part of the poem, *Lonicera sempervirens*, or
trumpet honeysuckle, is sent, as a herald, to call a
parley, and the parties meet on the plain of *Enna*,°
so much celebrated by the poets for its flowers and the
rape of Proserpina. *Flora* enters in a wheel-barrow,
the garden carriage, driving *Hyacinthus*, *Carnatia*,

*Auricula, Tulippa, Anemonia, Jonquilla, Ranunculus,*
and *Polyanthus,* eight in hand, and is attended by Cu-
pids, as gardeners, bearing silver cream-pots and all
the prizes given at florists' feasts. *Botania* is borne in
a tin box, the botanists' conveyance, by eight of her
favourites; and, after debating the matter, as we do
at Coachmakers' Hall,° which introduces an episode
upon that elegant amusement, it is agreed that they
shall henceforth unite their powers, and live promis-
cuously in fields or gardens: a pageant takes place,
in which all their adherents appear two and two, attended by Gnomes and Sylphs: Botania and Flora
change their cars, and a triumphal song is chanted to
their joint honour.

*Sir Charles.* How new and how truly poetic is the
idea!

*Ver.* You compliment.—But bless me! where is
Sir Charles? We had better be setting off.

*Sir Charles.* Which does your Ladyship mean?
For one was Sir Charles yesterday, and the other to-
day; like Archer and Aimwell,° they take it by turns,
I believe, to be master and servant.

*Ver.* How!

*Sir Charles.* Here comes the gentleman to speak
for himself. With your permission, I will wait upon
the young lady, and give her some farther insight into
your favourite science.

*Ver.* By all means. We will overtake you towards
Lowdore.                           [*Exit* Sir Charles.

*Enter* Speedwell, *in regimentals.*

*Speed.* Abashed with shame, I am come, most lovely of women, to implore your pardon, for an imposition which I have practised upon you.

*Ver.* How! Speedwell!

*Speed.* I am, Madam, the unhappy and the happy man who would no longer be thought Speedwell, but Sir Charles Portinscale. Willing to witness, unobserved by the lovely Beccabunga Veronica, those charms of which the world speaks so highly, but which I believed it impossible for mortal to be endowed with, I changed characters with my servant, and viewed them at humble distance. Who could see, and not love? Have pity upon me then, and, in sealing my doom, remember that my death follows your refusal, and my happiness your gracious condescension.

*Ver.* And so you really think I have so little penetration as not to know you?

*Speed.* I hope so. (*Aside.*)

*Ver.* Is it possible that the accomplishments of Sir Charles Portinscale could really be concealed under the appearance of a menial?

*Speed.* She has not discovered us, I hope. (*Aside.*)

*Ver.* No, Sir Charles, I have more penetration than that: though you seem to think not, by attempting to pass your vulgar, illiterate servant upon me as yourself. That chivalric air of yours is not to be imitated. I can assure you I was not insensible to the dear "speechless messages" which I received from your eyes:° but you know, Sir Charles, if I had not given into it, I should have spoiled one of the best incidents that could possibly occur for my tour. It is a most picturesque incident, and perfectly classical. The heathen deities, you know, often changed their forms, to pursue their amours, and your royal namesake° travelled, like you, in disguise, secretly to witness the charms of his intended.

*Speed.* How amiable is this forgiving kindness! Yet, how shall I apologise for the insults offered by my servant?

*Ver.* O dear, don't mention them. His vulgarity and positivity were a little distressing; and, as I am not a *mesembryanthemum crystallinum,*° I could not forbear now and then showing a little spontaneity of scintillation: I am certainly phosphorescent, like the *Tropœolum;*° but your submission disarms me.

*Speed.* Unexampled goodness! Then let me hope that the flame which warms my heart is answered by a kindred blaze in yours.

*Ver.* Well, then, I will be equally frank with yourself: in short, Sir Charles, I am not willing to be solely female all my life, like the *caprifica.*° And what woman, when offered the hand of Sir Charles Portinscale, could refuse it?

*Speed.* O say, when will you complete my happiness? Were I to lose you—were you to alter your mind——

*Ver.* Never, Sir Charles—And to convince you—
——But money can be no object to you——Yet, Sir
Charles, I have a tolerable fortune, and, to convince
you of my love, I insist upon your taking a bond for
my forfeiting it all, in case of a refusal.

*Speed.* By no means. Recollect, I have once deceived you.

*Ver.* I beg you will not say so, Sir Charles; you
have not deceived me. I merely humoured the deception for the sake of the incident. If you refuse to
take it, Sir Charles, I shall think you are not sincere.
Here is pen, ink, and paper, and you shall have it
immediately. (*Sits down and writes.*)

*Speed.* Am I to blame for this? She makes love,
to her own ensnaring. (*Aside.*) But, Madam, how do
you know that I am not still an impostor? Are you
certain I am Sir Charles Portinscale? If hereafter you
should find I have deceived you——

*Ver.* Then blame me, and I'll forgive you. (*Gives
a bond.*) Do you think I could, even for a moment,
have encouraged that vulgar fellow, but out of regard
to his charming prototype? I declare, I remind myself
of *Collinsonia*:°

Two *brother swains, of* Collin*'s gentle name,*°
*The same their features, and their forms the same,*
*With rival love for fair* Collinia *sigh,*
*Knit the dark brow, and roll th'unsteady eye:*

*With sweet concern the pitying beauty mourns,*
*And sooths, with simpering smiles, the pair by turns.*

*Speed.* Accomplished charmer! How shall I repay this increasing debt of love?

*Ver.* Let us be walking, Sir Charles. Let me take your arm. From the soft voice of love we must turn to the sublime and terrible of nature: but, Sir Charles, I fear you do not love me?

*Speed.* Ne'er was vegetable love so constant to his mistress.

## AIR.

*When borne upon the buoyant air,*
Diœcius° *seeks his amorous fair,*
*O'er woods and wilds he takes his flight,*
*From early morn to latest night,*
*Sees thousand beauties round him rise,*
*Yet steers, with undiverted eyes,*
*Till, having found his fair-one's charms,*
*He rests within her peaceful arms.*

### Veronica.

*Thus* Vallisneria° *patient bides*
*The flowering of the welcome tides,*
*Which, as they onward gently move,*

*Bring her glad tidings of her love;*
*And, as the fragrant zephyrs sweep*
*The bosom of the swelling deep,*
*Her love appears in blooming charms,*
*And hastes to her expecting arms.*          [*Exeunt.*

## SCENE II.

*On the Banks of* Derwent-water.

*Enter* Sir Charles *and* Lydia.

*Lydia.* Though you have explained your motives,
Sir Charles, for this extraordinary conduct, and I,
in part, admit the justice of it; yet, be assured, I
never can bring myself to see my aunt ill treated or
exposed, notwithstanding her strange and harsh conduct towards me. Believe me, Sir Charles, the time I
pass with her, and the painful obligations which she
confers upon me, are almost too much for a mind not
stronger than my own.

*Sir Charles.* Then suffer me to release you from
your slavery, and confer an obligation upon me, by
taking your liberty at my hands.

## AIR.

*Thus when, unshelter'd, we expose*
*To wasting storms the blushing rose,*
*     It droops its lovely head:*
*Oppress'd by grief and fretting tears,*
*By slow degrees its beauty wears,*
*     And all its charms are fled.*

*But shake the wasting tears away,*
*And let it hail the solar ray,*
*     No more it meets the ground;*
*Again it lifts its lovely head,*
*With nature's choicest beauty spread,*
*     And breathes delight around.*

*Lydia.* Your generous conduct, Sir Charles, demands my warmest gratitude. You have been pleased to select me from amongst the thousands you have seen; and, not to be sensible of the honour, would betray a heart incapable of love or of reason. To become your wife will be my honour, as well as my happiness; yet, in accepting that, I must not forget, that, though I at times experience harsh treatment from my aunt, under whose care I am placed, till I become of age to be my own mistress, I am under many obligations to her; and, though no authority shall force me to an engagement against my own inclination, nor cruelty deprive me of the object of my affections, I will not buy my own happiness at the expense of hers, nor see her exposed without resenting it.

*Sir Charles.* How noble, to be thus solicitous for those who are unmindful of our welfare! To shield myself from the vain attacks of your aunt, has been the sole motive for these transformations. To prevent her from exposing herself, you yourself must well know is impossible. But if, in avoiding her attacks, and attempting to forward the great object of my happiness, I should be guilty of dishonour or injustice, may I, as my punishment, bring down the misery upon my own head, which I would have brought upon another.

*Lydia.* Then what is your design in thus continuing your disguise, and of the artifice of your servant?

*Sir Charles.* To gain time to secure the affections and the hand of my Lydia. But, were my servant even to prevail upon your aunt to accept him, my life on it! the man has worth to aspire to a nobler choice. He is my servant, and he is my friend.

*Lydia.* It is in your honour I confide.

*Sir Charles.* But I shall take you, Lydia, only from one strife to another, and from one tyranny to perhaps a greater restraint. Can you bear the inconvenience and the tumult of a camp, and the uncertainty and hazard of joining your fate with a soldier's?

*Lydia.* Yes, when that soldier generously joins his fate with mine.

## AIR.

*When the fife and the drum shall muster the band,*
  *And the troops all for marching prepare,*
*When you, at their head, give the word of command,*
  *And the trumpet's shrill clang rends the air:*

*With a heart beating high in response to their notes,*
  *Whilst their banners are flouting the wind,*
*And the full tide of war in the atmosphere floats,*
  *Pleas'd I'll follow in safety behind.*

*If the battle should rage, in the midst of the strife,*
  *To the guardians of Virtue I'll cry,*
*To restore you, unharm'd, to the arms of your wife,*
  *Or with you be permitted to die.*

*Sir Charles.* Then will my Lydia consent to entrust herself to my honour? A few hours will remove us to the place, where there can be no impediment to our union; and we may then return to your aunt without any farther apprehensions.

*Lydia.* By no means. Declare yourself at once, your title and your intentions. When she finds you resolved not to accept her, she will be proud in your alliance with me; and we shall not find any farther bars to our happiness.

## DUET.

*When two fond hearts in mutual love*
*Their fortunes firm unite,*
*Dear is the bliss they then approve,*
*Unruffled their delight:*

*For Reason then, with sanction wise,*
*Reveres their plighted troth,*
*And Angels, bending from the skies,*
*Are witness to their oath.*          [*Exeunt.*

## SCENE III.

*A Room at the Queen's Head.*

*Enter* Bob Kiddy, Anna Katharina, *and* Landlord.

*Bob.* Where are aunt and coz, and the captain?

*Landlord.* They are gone to Lowdore water-fall, Sir. There is a party in their room eating a sandwich; as soon as they are gone, Sir, I will show you up.

*Bob.* Yup-a-hey, Kate! Put down the things, and go about your business, my little galloper. I show'd you what good driving is, I think. I rode the horse myself, drove post: rather a crack-thing that.

*Landlord.* A gentleman be his own post boy! (*Aside.*)

*Anna.* Kate! my name's Anna Katharina.

*Bob.* You are aunt's Anna Katharina, as you call yourself, but you are my Kate; and a sweet cate° you are too.

*Landlord.* I'll show the young woman to my wife.

*Anna.* Young woman! Anna Katharina, Sir.

[*Exit with* Landlord.

*Bob.* Gone to see the water-fall! that's rum enough. I'll see a good stream of wine before the day's out. Must have a sandwich before dinner. Was rather peckish at breakfast—cropsick from last night. Here, waiter. (*Enter* Landlord.) Must have a sandwich and a draught of porter. Have you got a tennis-court here?

*Landlord.* No, Sir.

*Bob.* Or a billiard-table?

*Landlord.* No, Sir.

*Bob.* Not a billiard-table! Why, I never knew such a place in my life. Not a billiard-table! Has any body got a bear, or a badger to bait? or fighting cocks? Famous fun that.—Like to see 'em challenge: cock, cock, cock, cock, coo. (*Imitates cocks.*) Then they peck the ground, and come on in a style.——Deadly fine fun is a Welsh main.°

*Landlord.* Deadly indeed, Sir; for it costs many

poor creatures their lives.—No, Sir, we have nothing of that kind here.—This is some cruel coward.
(*Aside.*)

*Bob.* Why, how do people pass their time here?
What have you got to eat?

*Landlord.* The lady ordered dinner at four. There
is some of the red trout——

*Bob.* Plague on't, the bottle of fish sauce was
broken when the Sociable came down. I never travel
without fish sauce. The chow-chow° is all gone too.

*Landlord.* A leg of nice mutton, Sir——

*Bob.* Let's have some currant-jelly with it.

*Landlord.* And a couple of roast fowls.

*Bob.* Broil one of 'em, and pepper it well. Make
a devil° of it, and let's have the best wine in your
cellar.

*Landlord.* And then you'll make a devil of yourself. (*Aside.*) It shall be as you order, Sir. We've a
nice grouse in the pantry, Sir.

*Bob.* Does it stink?

*Landlord.* As sweet as a nut, Sir.

*Bob.* Then keep it till it does, for then aunt and
coz won't touch it; and I shall have it all to myself.
Bring me a glass of cherry brandy, and get me a sandwich.

*Landlord.* Directly, Sir. We've some nice hung
beef in the house.                              [*Exit.*

## SONG.

### Bob.

*Let others travel far and near,*
*To view each hill and valley,*
*To see how different scenes appear,*
*And wherein 'tis they tally:*
*My purpose is where I begin*
*To see each country's produce,*
*To tell the merits of each inn,*
*And what I find of no use.*

*The ruin'd castle some admire,*
*Which lets in wind and weather;*
*I like the snug and blazing fire,*
*When shelter'd altogether.*
*And though a lake is well enough*
*For sailing or for rowing,*
*I better like the right good stuff*
*That sets me off a rouing.°*

*Some ninnies go around the world*
*In search of fine adventures,*
*From port to port by weather hurl'd,*
*Till all their fortune's spent thus.*
*From port to port too I will go,*
*From Teneriffe to Lisbon;*
*And so of wine I get enow,*
*Why faith to me it is one.*

*Enter* Landlord, *with First and Second* Pedestrian, *dressed in sailor's jackets and trowsers, knapsacks at their backs, umbrellas, &c.*

*Landlord.* Two gentlemen on foot, Sir. Your room will be ready immediately.                    [*Exit.*

*Bob.* Foot! Poor devils!

*1st Ped.* We do not interrupt you, I hope, Sir?

*Bob.* No. What you've walked, have you? Why do you walk as sailors?

*1st Ped.* The dress is light, and well adapted for travelling.

*Bob.* But a'n't you afraid of being taken up?

*2d Ped.* No, Sir. We injure no one, why should any one injure us?

*Bob.* You must be a little tired and foot-sore, I think?

*1st Ped.* Neither, Sir; we are used to it, and suffer no inconvenience whatever.

*Bob.* Used to it! What, you've come some way?

*2d Ped.* Some hundreds of miles, Sir.

*Bob.* What, going home? or going to see your friends?

*2d Ped.* Neither, Sir! Travelling for pleasure.

*Bob.* That's a good one! Travelling on foot for pleasure!

*1st Ped.* Yes, Sir.

*Bob.* Short of cash, perhaps? But then you might have staid at home.

*2d Ped.* But not have seen the world there. My friend and myself, being anxious to see other places besides our own, and other men and other manners than those of our own confined circle, travel thus, at a light expense, in search of knowledge and amusement.

*Bob.* Why, they're crack'd. What then, if you had money, you wouldn't walk?

*2d Ped.* Not altogether that, Sir. We might perhaps afford what others might esteem accommodations, but which would be none to us.

*Bob.* I wouldn't give a penny to travel without horses and servants.

*1st Ped.* That involves a great expense. But, in not having them, we have fewer troubles, and secure our independance. A horse requires care and attendance; he may knock up, he may fall lame: a servant will scarcely live upon less than a moderate gentleman; he will not perhaps submit to the fatigue, he may impose upon you, he may cheat you, he may be impertinent. Our own feelings tell us when we should rest, and when we should go on; we carry the slight changes we want at our backs; we stand in need of no other service, and have no trouble nor inconvenience respecting our conveyance; it is always ready when we are, and rest repairs any slight injury it may undergo during the day, and they which carry us are always comfortably lodged when we are. Exercise secures appetite and sleep; the contemplation of the works of nature and of man affords amusement and exercise to the mind, and health results from both.

## AIR.

### First Ped.

*In viewing Nature's varied scenes,*
*Sweet is the pleasure they impart,*
*For Reason scarce has better means*
*To soften and improve the heart.*

### Second Ped.

*From exercise what spirits flow!*
*Sweet is the meal that Hunger finds,*
*And sweet the slumbers that we know,*
*The calm repose of tranquil minds.*

### Both.

*Then let us range the vallies still,*
*And o'er the mountain's summit wind,*
*Trace with delight the gurgling rill,*
*And still preserve the tranquil mind.*

*Bob.* Quizical enough! travel for health and improvement! Why, I never care about either. Aunt gazes about her, to be sure; but I never look at any thing but the stables and the larder. And what have you learnt, pray?

*2d Ped.* We have learnt, Sir, that human nature
is pretty much the same in every place and in every
condition. All ranks have their pleasures and their
pains, their virtues and their vices. My Lord risks
his guineas at faro, and the clown his halfpence at
chuck.° My Lord gets drunk with wine, and murders
his friend in a duel; the clown gets intoxicated with
ale, he quarrels with his pot companion, and breaks
his rib, or beats out an eye in a boxing-bout; if he does
not murder him, it is the difference of the weapons,
not the superior virtue of the clown, which spares
him. Miss dances at the ball, and the next morning elopes with the captain; the country lass dances
her jig at the fair with her sweetheart, and the next
morning has as little honesty as her superior in rank.
My Lord profanes his sabbath at the card-table or
the concert, the clown at tossing-up,° or in the ale-
house. If the *rich* do not *seek* opportunities of doing
good, the *poor neglect* them when they occur. It is
certain we have all our vices, and I hope we have all
some virtues.

*Bob.* I should think now you might pick up something as you travel, by preaching from the top of a
beer-barrel, or from a hollow tree. Come, I'll treat
you with a bottle of wine a-piece, if you like it, and
give you a bit of dinner into the bargain.

*1st Ped.* We thank you, Sir, for your offer, but
beg leave to decline it.

*Bob.* Well, I don't understand you two together.

Refuse a bottle of wine!  If you'd offer me two, I'd drink 'em both.

*1st Ped.*    Every thing with us depends upon health, and we must not risk that by intemperance. Nor is it for people in our situation to pay three and sixpence a bottle for wine.  Without wine we can travel better; and, what is more, we can travel farther.

*Bob.*  Why, you starve yourselves.

*2d Ped.*  That would be as bad, Sir.  No, Sir, we live well, but plain: and in a draught of good ale we find more health and nourishment, than in the liquid fire retailed in bottles at an inn.

*Bob.*  Well, I find I can make nothing of you, and so good bye.——Of all the quizzes° I've ever seen, commend me to your pedestrians. (*Aside, and exit.*)

*1st Ped.*  Well, Frank, we'll treat *ourselves* with a bit of dinner, and then for the wonders of Keswick.

*2d Ped.*  With all my heart.            [*Exeunt.*

## SCENE IV.

*The Village of* Grange *in* Borrowdale.
*—Haymakers making hay.*

*Enter* Veronica, Speedwell, Lydia, *and* Sir Charles.


*Ver.* What delightful scenes of pastoral and syl-
van simplicity, contrasted with the terrific mountains
which surround them! They remind me of the days of
Arcadian innocence. These peaceful cots, sequestered
in the gloom of beech and sycamore, form an umbrageous landscape, which, set off by the empurpling
and downy hue of the clouds, with occasional inter-
ventions of gay gleams of light, are so many circumstances of imagery, which give a magical effect to the
whole, well according with my solemn tone of feeling
at this moment. I am afraid, Sir Charles, I may be
tautologous; but it is scarcely possible, in repeated
descriptions, to avoid it. Pray, Mr. Botanist, have
you any of the *persicaria siliquosa*, or *noli me tangere*,° growing hereabouts? It is one of the few plants
I am unacquainted with.

*Sir Charles.* The *touch me not*! It is found in
great plenty near Windermere. It is a pity that your
Ladyship is so entirely unacquainted with it, as it is a
curious plant, and well worthy your attention.—This,
Madam, is the delightful village of Grange, celebrated

for its hospitality to Mr. Gray;° and this the gorge of Borrowdale, whose terrible appearance intimidated him from exploring farther these finest of scenes.

*Ver.* Don't speak, lest the agitation of the air should loosen the rocks above, and bring down a mass that would overwhelm us.

*Speed.* Many a person, Madam, has brought ruin upon himself by speaking, when he should have held his tongue.——And, though ruin should hang over her head, sooner than hold her tongue, a woman e'en lets it have its own way. (*Aside.*)

*Ver.* A fine opportunity for a peep into pastoral life, and an incident to secure Sir Charles's heart for ever. (*Aside.*) Sir Charles, my heart beats in fond sympathy with the innocence of these uncorrupted mountaineers—

*Speed.* Their innocence is of a very singular nature then. (*Aside.*)

*Ver.* To eat oat-cake and butter-milk in the peaceful mansion—I have got some tongue in my pocket.

*Speed.* Yes, she always carries a tongue with her. (*Aside.*)

*Ver.* Give me your arm.

*Speed.* You had better not give way to this amiable sensibility: let me lead you back to the hotel at Lowdore.

*Ver.* Not for the world—my too susceptible heart—

*Speed.* It is susceptible, I believe, of *twice* as much

as any other. (*Aside.*)

*Sir Charles.* Hard by is the habitation of an hospitable herdsman; his door is ever open to those who will please to enter it.

## AIR.

*Beneath the tall beech that grows hard by the tide,*
*Will Hearty, a plain honest soul, does reside;*
*He's a friend to the rich, he's a friend to the poor,*
*For ne'er on distress hath he yet shut his door.*

*He's a board that is spread with his plain wholesome*
*And a cellar affording a jug of good beer;      [fare,*
*If themselves Thirst or Hunger before him present,*
*Will Hearty will always their wishes prevent.°*

*But if by the rich or the noble he's sought,*
*The choicest of dainties before him are brought,*
*And, while they thus honour his plain friendly board,*
*Will Hearty is happy, and great as a lord.*

*Ver.* Lead me there. Oh, Sir Charles! these overcoming scenes of the grand and the sublime—

*Speed.* Let me draw your veil over your eyes, and you won't see them—

*Ver.* Lead me into the peaceful cot—Oh!— (*Faints.*)

*Speed.* Mr. Guide, assist me with the lady.

*Sir Charles.* This way, if you please: here, under the lowly shed of poverty, we shall find the princely virtue of compassion, and get assistance to recover this amiable absentee—That sentence must, I think, be put down in the tour. (*Aside.*)——Madam, may we desire your assistance?

*Lydia.* No doubt my aunt will soon recover: a bit of oat-cake and a draught of butter-milk will awaken her from this transitory trance.            [*Exeunt.*

*Haymakers come forward.*

*Haymaker.* Come, my lads and lasses, the day is warm, and labour makes us thirsty; a draught of beer will refresh us. Bring the keg, and we'll sing a roundel as it circulates.

### AIR *and* CHORUS.

*The southern breeze that through the dale,*
*While new-mown meadows sweets exhale,*
   *Breathes fragrance and delight around:*
*While upward soars the shrill-gorg'd lark,*
*The village swains attentive hark,*
   *And catch the cheerful sound:*
*With him they hail the sun's bright ray,*
*And labour cheerly through the day.*

END OF THE SECOND ACT.

# ACT III.

## SCENE I.

*A Room at the Queen's Head.*

*Enter* Sample *and* Anna.

### *Anna.*

I DESIRES, Sir, you won't follow me about so: I thought ye had been a gentleman; but, as ye be only a gentleman's gentleman, ye be not for my money, I can assure ye: besides, ye don't understand botamy.

*Sample.* No, how should I?

*Anna.* Oh, such an enlightened study! such hard names! Why, do you know I was a whole day larning a single word, and forgot it again the next morning. Another word, to be sure, I larnt in an hour; but then I forgot it the next minute. But my mistress recollects every thing; she is a great schollard. Such curious truths too contained in it—why, plants are all men and women.

*Sample.* Aye, there are sweet-williams; I'm a sweet-william. And coxcombs, and painted ladies, and lords and ladies, and naked ladies, like your modern fine ladies, and—

*Anna.* No, no, I mean that they drink and sleep, and are like man and wife.

*Sample.* What, sleep in the same bed?

*Anna.* Yes, and in different beds, and live sometimes in different houses.

*Sample.* Have a separate *maintainance*! They must be your fashionable plants then. What, and some have their misses, I reckon, as well as their wives?

*Anna.* O yes! a great many: and some ladies have their gallants too.

*Sample.* Upon my word, Miss, a very pretty study this seems to be that you've learnt: I can't say I should much like my wife to know any thing about it.

*Anna.* That you'll find a difficult matter to get one who's ignorant of it; for all ladies that know any thing study botamy now: and, if I hadn't despised ye before, I do now for your ignorance.

*Sample.* And yet, I don't know, I like her very well; and if she'll make a good wife in other respects, I'll take care she doesn't get to her gallants, and to living in a different house. (*Aside.*) Now, if I was to love you, and give you a proof of my love?

*Anna.* I can't like nobody that isn't larned.

*Sample.* It seems to be the way to get wives by telling lies: I'm telling a lie by saying I'm a sarvant, and one lie isn't worse than another. (*Aside.*) Now suppose I was really a gentleman, and only made myself a sarvant to see if I liked you? Suppose I was a baronet?

*Anna.* A what!

*Sample.* Suppose I was Sir Charles Portinscale, and disguised myself to see how I liked you, and win your heart?

*Anna.* Sir Charles Portinscale, that danced with my young mistress at Lancaster?

*Sample.* And liked you better than she, and so told her I was a sarvant, to get away from her.

*Anna.* Why, you don't say so? And she wouldn't have ye, because ye was a sarvant? A proud minx!

*Sample.* But don't you say a word about it.

*Anna.* And so you really love me?—This comes now to my young lady for not knowing the sensual* system. He likes me best, though he don't know why. (*Aside.*) And do you mean to marry me, Sir Charles? I've got some money, I can assure you; I've saved two hundred pounds in sarvice.

*Sample.* Just serve to set me up in a nice little shop of my own. (*Aside.*) To be sure I do. But you mustn't now say any thing to any body about it. We'll be married directly.

*Anna.* And then I shall really be a lady?

*Sample.* Yes, you'll be my lady.

*Anna.* And you won't be ashamed of owning me?

---

* Called by botanists sexual.

*Sample.* No, if you leave off your strange talk about men and women, and misses and gallants.

*Anna.* Aye, that I will.—A woman never thinks any promise she makes at marriage binding. (*Aside.*)

*Sample.* Well, then let's break a sixpence upon it. Come.

## AIR.

### Sample.

*This sixpence break*
*For my dear sake;*
 *'Twill join our hearts together:*
*As sure as fate,*
*You're then my Kate,*
 *In matrimonial tether.*

### Anna.

*I hold it true,*
*When broke in two,*
 *Our hearts in one combine-a;*
*But 'tis not fate*
*Can make me Kate,*
 *I'm Anna Katharina.*

*Anna.* There, it's a match. (*They break a six-pence.*)

*Enter* Bob Kiddy.

*Bob.* What's a match, my little puss?

*Anna.* Match! O dear—why only for me and my fellow-sarvant to play a game at cards.

*Bob.* Your fellow-sarvant! Why, it's the officer that brought aunt and coz. What, you're a poacher, Captain?

*Sample.* I mustn't tell him who I am. (*Aside to* Anna.) I'm no Captain, Sir, but the Captain's man.

*Bob.* No! Why, you'd regimentals on when you took up aunt and coz.

*Sample.* Had I? O aye! My master desired me to wear his cloathes to air them.

*Bob.* That's a lie, I believe.

*Sample.* Do you give me the lie, Sir?

*Bob.* No, I don't say it *is* a lie; only that *I believe* it is one.

*Sample.* I believe he's only a bully. I'll frighten him. (*Aside.*) Why then, you lie, Sir.

*Bob.* I believe he daresn't fight, though he talks so big. He's no great shakes, I think. (*Aside.*) Do you give me the lie, Sir?

*Sample.* No; you take it to yourself. If you'd given me the lie, I'd have pull'd you by the nose.—I fancy I'm as strong as he. (*Aside.*)

*Bob.* You should fight me if you was a gentleman; but, as you are only a servant, I shall cane you.

*Sample.* But I am a gentleman. I am the officer.

*Bob.* Then you've told a lie, in saying you was his servant.

*Sample.* Do you tell me then that I lie?

*Bob.* No; you tell yourself so. But you gave me the lie, and shall fight me.

*Sample.* I do know something of sparring. Come on, then.

*Bob.* Why, you blackguard! You don't think I'll box with you? You shall fight me with pistols.

*Sample.* So, now I've got into another scrape. I don't think he dare fire. (*Aside.*) Very well, I'm not afraid.

*Bob.* He must be though, by saying he's not. (*Aside.*) Well then, get a second, and I'll meet you.

*Sample.* Why, he's my second, for I've escaped fighting with one before.—I'll get Speedwell to go with me, and perhaps he won't let us fight. (*Aside.*) Very well, I'm your man.

*Anna.* No—No—you mustn't fight. If you kill him, you'll kill—Oh!—Oh!—Oh! (*Sobbing.*)

*Sample.* Aye, she'll take care to prevent us. (*Aside.*) I'll be with you in a crack. You've insulted my honour, and must satisfy me.          [*Exit.*

*Bob.* I'll kill him, if that will be any satisfaction to him. But it'll not be any to me to be kill'd. I'd better not have provoked him. For though he may be only a bully, yet he may fight, and he may kill me.—Well! that's a good thought.——I know what I'll do, and then I shall be sure to be safe. Here come the pedestrians. I'll get one of them to be my second, perhaps he'll make it up.

*Enter* Pedestrians.

Well, my lads, how are you? I'm glad to see you again. So you wouldn't crack a bottle with me? Well; now I want you to do me a good turn.

*Anna.* Oh! you bloodthirsty brute! I'll have you bound over to your good behaviour.

*1st Ped.* That would be no very easy matter, I believe.

*Anna. (Sobbing.)* But he sha'n't fight. I'll go and I'll——He's only a sarvant, and he's no right to be killed as a gentleman.

## AIR.

*Oh dear, my heart I'm sure will break!*
*If you away his life should take,*
*Then all my hopes are gone;*
*For then my days, ah! I'm afraid,*
*I shall be forc'd to pass a maid,*
*And never cease to mourn.*          [*Exit.*

*1st Ped.* What is the cause of this, Sir? A woman in tears, and you not attempt to dry them!

*Bob.* Why, I'm going to kill her sweetheart, I believe, and I want you to assist me.

*1st Ped.* Kill her sweetheart, and want me to assist you!

*Bob.* Yes, I'm going to fight him, and want you to be my second.

*1st Ped.* Fight a duel, and wish me to be your second! No, Sir.

*Bob.* Why, you a'n't afraid, are you?

*1st Ped.* I am, Sir. I am afraid to break the laws of my country and my Maker.

*Bob.* But a man of honour doesn't care for either. Besides, if I should kill him, the coroner's inquest will only bring it in "manslaughter;" or if they should bring it in "murder," depend upon it we can manage to have a flaw in the indictment.

*1st Ped.* And, Sir, would you implicate me in a crime, for which I may run the hazard of my own life?

*Bob.* Why, you're only to be my second. I don't want to fight you.

*1st Ped.* But he, Sir, who looks on, and calmly beholds his fellow-creatures commit murder, is accessary to the crime, and must answer it to his offended country with his life.

*Bob.* He talks very fine. He's my man. I'm sure, if I press him, he'll put a stop to it. (*Aside.*) Well, but you wouldn't mind your life for a friend?

*1st Ped.* A friend! You offered me a bottle of wine! Sir, for a true friend, nay, in a good cause, I would risk my life for my enemy; but I will not hazard it in being second in a duel.

*Bob.* But he gave me the lie.

*1st Ped.* I would not have *accepted* the ill language of one, who so little knew what good breeding was.

*Bob.* But he threatened to pull my nose. What can I do in that case?

*1st Ped.* If you really fear, go with your nose soaped.

*Bob.* Why, he's laughing at me. I can tell you, Sir, I can always laugh at those that laugh at me.

*1st Ped.* Then, Sir, you are the laughing philosopher, and laugh at the whole world. You must lead a very merry life.

*Bob.* Yes, pretty well for that. I keep it up. So you won't stand my friend?

*1st Ped.* What is it you want, Sir?

*Bob.* I want satisfaction, and you to see that I have it.

*1st Ped.* Will it be any satisfaction to you to be killed?

*Bob.* No.

*1st Ped.* Or to kill your adversary?

*Bob.* Yes.

*1st Ped.* Malignant spirit! By being second I may prevent extremities. (*Aside.*) Well, Sir, if you desire it, though I do not consider you as having any claim upon me more than another, I will accompany you, and see the matter adjusted. Where is your antagonist, and when and where do you meet?

*Bob.* Gone to look for a second — in the fields — directly.——Perhaps your companion will be second to the other?

*2d Ped.* If he desires it, I will accompany him.

*Bob.* Well, that shows some pluck. I'll go tell him, and get the pistols, and we'll have it out directly.

[*Exit.*

*2d Ped.* Well, Ned, we must act the part which good seconds should always play, not urge, but compose the differences of the principals. If I can judge rightly, this Hector,° though he talks big, does not much relish the business. But he seems to be a bully, and against such we must ever be upon our guard.

## AIR.

*What a monster is man! that he'd rather revenge,*
*Than be great, though he's meek, and forgive;*
*His heart from his friend, for one word he'll estrange,*
*And forbid him to friendship to live.*

### First Ped.

*Revenge is a dæmon, the missive of hell;*
*But Forgiveness, an Angel from heaven,*
*Teaches best how mankind may in happiness dwell,*
*And forgive, as we would be forgiven.*

## Both.

*Then come, thou mild Angel, by fortitude arm'd,*
*And resist the proud claims of thy foe,*
*And while at the pow'r of thy might he's alarm'd,*
*Hurl him down to his region below.*     [*Exeunt.*

## SCENE II.

*Another Room.*

*Enter* Lydia.

*Lydia.* My fate, I hope, is now drawing towards a crisis. Sir Charles will assert his cause and my own, and relieve me from the irksome situation I am in with my aunt.

## AIR.

*Though envy distresses,*
*And pride oft oppresses,*
    *And lays all our happiness waste;*
*Yet powerful love*
*Ev'ry care will remove,*
    *And on high rear his banner at last.*

*Enter* Veronica.

*Ver.* Well Lydia, my dear, Sir Charles is oblig-
ingly gone with the botanist to look for the *Geranium batrachoides flore eleganter variegato*;° he has
promised to get me two or three roots to put into
pots, for me to take back for the garden at Diandria Hall.———A vastly agreeable man is that Sir
Charles. I don't think you admire him so much as
you did. You were quite enraptured with him at Lancaster, but now you seem quite indifferent.

*Lydia.* You accused me, Madam, of insensibility
towards the Sir Charles Portinscale, who brought us
hither in his carriage.

*Ver.* A very pleasant and picturesque scheme was
that of Sir Charles's. Yes, I had a mind to humour
it, to give it effect. How easy, how polite, how enlightened is Sir Charles! how rich too in the language
of botany! The soul-expanding delight of an inter-
communication of sentiments with Sir Charles, when
put in contradistinction with the obscuration of in-
tellect in that prominently disagreeable man, that *roturier*,° his servant, is like the *rosa provincialis* com-
pared with the *allium roseum*.°

*Lydia.* I have little reason to be partial to the gentleman, as he seems to have no partiality to me. His
attentions are directed to you, Madam. It remains
with you, therefore, to encourage or oppose them.

*Ver.* Upon my word! a little jealous or so! Sir

Charles has discernement, Miss; and, if he prefers an enlightened mind to one not yet emerged from primitive darkness and prejudice, surely he is to make his own election where he thinks proper.

*Lydia.* Certainly, Madam.

*Ver.* And if Sir Charles would die, were I to be cruel, a truly philanthropic heart will bid him live to love and happiness. Yes, you will, before very long, be niece to Lady Beccabunga Portinscale; when the new plant the botanist has found will be called the Portinscalia.

*Lydia.* If it is Sir Charles's and your wish, I have neither a right nor a cause to wish it otherwise.

*Ver.* Vastly obliging indeed! But I have been so presumptuous as absolutely to consent to the hymeneal union, without previously asking your permission.

*Lydia.* You are then engaged, Madam?

*Ver.* Beyond the possibility of retreating, but with the consent of Sir Charles.

*Lydia.* I had no right to expect it; but perhaps, Madam, it had been better had you consulted me.

*Ver.* Astonishing impertinence! Yes, Miss, and you may, if you like it, for I give you my free leave, go and marry his servant; or, perhaps, I may give you leave to marry the botanist. Yes, you may marry him.

*Lydia.* I thank you, Madam, for your goodness.

*Enter* Anna.

*Anna.* O dear, Madam, I must beg your interposance: there is going to be such a confusion of blood yonder.

*Ver.* Blood! Where?

*Anna.* At the foot of Skiddaw.

*Ver.* They could not have chosen a more picturesque situation. But who is it?

*Anna.* My young master.

*Ver.* Bob! A silly blockhead! What business has he to be fighting? However, I'll introduce him in the foreground of a sketch by way of a memorandum.

*Lydia.* Dear me, Madam, let us go: our presence, the presence of women, will prevent their proceeding to extremities.

*Ver.* Interfere in a duel! It would absolutely class us amongst the *arums*\*: we should be *ara maculata.*°

*Lydia.* Consider, Madam, that by refusing our interference, where our presence might prevent a duel, we become parties in it, and shall have to reproach ourselves with any accident which may happen to either my cousin Robert or his antagonist.

*Ver.* Methinks, Miss, you are a little too much gifted with *verbiage.* Besides, were I to honour their combat with my presence, it would be, like one of the damsels of former times, to honour the conqueror with my gracious smiles.

\* Masculine ladies.

*Lydia.* How do you know but his antagonist may be Sir Charles Portinscale?

*Ver.* Bob dare as soon fight Tippoo Saib.°

*Anna.* It is, it is Sir Charles Portinscale.

*Lydia.* Heavens! Sir Charles! Perhaps it is only——but the uncertainty is dreadful. (*Aside.*) O let us haste this instant.

*Ver.* How, Sir Charles! Lead me to the place. Oh, that I were *papilionaceous*\*. I run to his protection, and let the fate-fraught tube discharge its leaden death into my breast before it lodges in his manly heart.

*Anna.* But hadn't you better take a constable?——

*Ver.* Vulgar expedient! No! I will be the mediator, the protector, and the deliverer: I perceive my love is growing *acumenate*:°

> *Arm'd in my virgin innocence I fly,*
> *My noble lover to protect or die.*°      [*Exeunt.*

---

\* Flowers are called *papilionaceous* whose petals are like the wings of a butterfly.

## SCENE III.

*The Foot of Skiddaw.*

*Enter* Speedwell.

*Speed.* I have counterfeited love till I have almost persuaded myself into a real passion for this woman, and I now dread the discovery, lest it should separate me from her for ever. But, suppose she should like me, and even consent to marry me, would I have her? She is rich, she is good tempered: two qualities that will certainly promote happiness in the married state. She does not want sense; but then she misapplies it. But it is perhaps for want of having it better directed, and the cares of a family may divert her attention another way. Then she is a botanist, and deeply versed in the mysteries of the loves of the plants; and she, who is bawd to a blossom, may not be very nice in the intercourse of her own species. I must have done with reflection, for the more I think the more I am bewildered.

## AIR.

*Like the false light, that o'er the moor*
*The 'nighted traveller beguiles,*
*Woman exerts her artful power*
*To lure you with her wanton smiles.*

*A ray of hope first faintly gleams,*
*    To cheer you on the lonely way,*
*And leads you on in airy dreams,*
*    At last your footsteps to betray.*

*You follow fast through bush and brake,*
*    And force with pain the tangled brier,*
*In hopes at last, for her dear sake,*
*    To gain the haven you desire.*

*But ah! at once in air dispers'd,*
*    The false and fickle beauty turns;*
*And he, each ray of comfort lost,*
*    His hapless fate despairing mourns.*

*Enter* Sir Charles Portinscale.

*Sir Charles.* Speedwell, look yonder. Is not that Veronica's nephew coming this way, with a man in a sailor's jacket; and, a little behind, Sample, with another in the same dress?

*Speed.* As sure as a gun it is, Sir, and they've got pistols with them. Perhaps they are coming hither to fight a duel.

*Sir Charles.* Let us step aside and observe them. (*They retire.*)

*Enter* Bob Kiddy *and* First Pedestrian.

*Bob.* No, I won't hear of an apology. I'll make him fight me.

*1st Ped.* Since you are determined, Sir, recollect that, as chance may equally go against you, as in your favour, whether there is any thing you wish to say, or any affairs you wish to be settled, should you fall.

*Bob.* Should I fall! No.

*1st Ped.* If you speak, Sir, from a consciousness of being prepared for the worst, happy is it for you. But the business you are upon, I fear, precludes any such favourable interpretation.

*Bob.* Why you don't mean to insult me, do you? for, if you do, here's a brace of pistols, and stand your ground.

*1st Ped.* Why you would not fight your second, Sir, would you? The friend who risks his life with yours!

*Bob.* If you risk it one way, why not another? But I won't put up with any such words.

*1st Ped.* Then, Sir, you must swallow them down.


*Enter* Sample *and* Second Pedestrian.

*Sample.* There he is, speak to him.

*2d Ped.* I would fain, Sir, terminate this affair amicably, if it be possible.

*Bob.* But it's impossible.

*2d Ped.* Then I beg to speak a word aside with your second.

*Bob.* Come, come, no collusion.

*Sample.* I see they won't let us fight. (*The* Pedestrians *walk aside,* Bob *and* Sample *look at each other.*)

*Bob.* Why you don't think I'll let you fight with those great horse-pistols, do you?

*Sample.* I thought I should frighten him. (*Aside.*)

*Bob.* Here, I've got two pair; you shall take a pair of mine: here.

*Sample.* No, I won't. How do I know but you've loaded 'em with slugs.

*Bob.* I believe you've done that yourself, by suspecting me. (Pedestrians *come forward.*)

*1st Ped.* If there is any difference respecting the weapons, it is our business to adjust it.

*Bob.* No. Only I won't let him fire with those horse-pistols. We must both have the same sort; and so he shall take a pair of mine. I've got two pair.—Here.

*2d Ped.* But this gentleman seems to suspect they may not be fairly loaded. Let me see.

*Bob.* No, you sha'n't. I believe his are not. Let me see them.

*Sample.* No, you sha'n't.

*1st Ped.* I have a right to insist in behalf of my principal.

*2d Ped.* And I of mine.

*1st Ped.* Give me your pistols, Sir.

*Sample.* There. Oh, dear!

*1st Ped.* Why, there is no ball in either of them.

*Sample.* No, I thought I would not shoot him: I only wanted to frighten him.

*2d Ped.* And now give me yours, if you please, Sir. (Bob *gives one pair*)—Come, gentlemen, I see you neither of you bore the other any ill-will, for these have no ball neither.

*Sample.* Well, that's very good-natured of you.— Come, let's shake hands.

*Bob.* With all my heart.

*2d Ped.* Stop, Sir. Just for the satisfaction of all parties, let us examine the other pair.

*Bob.* No, they are just the same.

*1st Ped.* Nay, Sir, if you hesitate, we must insist upon it. (*Takes them from him.*)—Loaded! These are what you would have retained yourself, and the un-loaded you would have forced upon your antagonist. Infamous, treacherous murderer!

*Bob.* Why, 'twas the only way of fighting to my own satisfaction:—but I'm off.

*2d Ped.* Not so soon, Sir. This must not stop here.

*Ver. (Without.)* Bob! Bob! Bob! If you fire, I will disinherit you. O Sir Charles——

*Enters with* Lydia *and* Anna.

——What, Bob and Speedwell! And has my intense solicitude been about my booby of a nephew and this odious *bourgeois* of a servant? Provoking!—there, you may fight it out. (*Looking about her.*) A most delightful spot! The road hither was enchanting; passing through bowery lanes, luxuriant with beech, birch, mountain-ash, and holly.—That *ravine* is extremely picturesque—that hill, covered with heath, turf, and browsing sheep—the road serpentising under that gnarled oak, with its tinty foliage—those beautiful boles, and that delicious distant dippy-dell——

Sir Charles *and* Speedwell *come forward.*

O my dear Sir Charles! I have had such multifarious palpitations on your account. (*To* Speedwell.)

*Lydia.* I was anxious, Sir Charles, for your safety; though I trusted it was not you who was involved in the duel. (*To* Sir Charles.)

*Anna.* I am all of a trimble, and all on your account, Sir Charles. (*To* Sample.)

*Bob.* How do you do, Sir Charles? Are you pretty hearty? (*To* Sir Charles.)

*Ver.* Hey! how is this! Sir Charles! Sir Charles! Sir Charles!

*Sir Charles.* Sir, I have witnessed your infamous conduct, and disclaim your acquaintance.

*Ver.* Why, what has he been doing?

*Sir Charles.* Was about to fire at his adversary with balls, when he had given him pistols with only powder in them.

*Ver.* A poltroon! How unlike the picturesque virtues of the ancients! when they met upon equal terms, shook hands, and fought for honour and renown.

*Speed.* This comes, Sir, of "seeking the bubble reputation at the pistol's mouth."°

*Sir Charles.* Bubble, indeed! for it is blown upon, and burst in air.

*Ver.* Sir Charles, as a military man, tell me what is to be done: for this story will get abroad, and I must give a full and perspicacious account of it in my tour.

*Speed.* It is not for me to speak in this instance. I refer you to that gentleman.

*Ver.* That gentleman!

*Sir Charles.* If it were not for the presence of these ladies, I should give you the chastisement due to a coward.

*Ver.* I beg that may be no objection. Besides, by being witness to it, I can give a more authenticated enarration, and more fully explain the chain of cause and effect. Oh, Bob! Bob! He ought to be made to pass *sub jugum.*°

*Sir Charles.* Have you nothing to say for yourself, Sir?

*Bob.* No: I am spiflicated!°

*Sir Charles.* Withdraw. Your own despicable cowardice, and the presence of these ladies, alone prevent me from giving you the caning you merit.

*Bob.* I am much obliged to the ladies and myself.

*Ver.* Bob, you don't enter my Sociable again.

*Sample.* No; he's not a sociable man.

*Bob.* I've no resource left but to turn tail upon the world, declaim against its vices, and set up myself as a pattern of every thing that's great and good. [*Exit.*

*Ver.* Pray, Mr. Speedwell, how came you engaged in a duel with my nephew? Was it a duel prepensed,° or a fortuitous collision?

*Sir Charles.* Matters, Madam, are too much involved at this moment to be but partially adjusted. That gentleman's name is not Speedwell, nor is he a servant. He is a TRAVELLER, with whom I by chance changed cloathes, and who, having his own pursuits interrupted, by my having his articles of trade, assumed the name and title of Sir Charles Portinscale, thinking therewith to make his fortune.

*Ver.* What! have I been made love to by a bagman?—What a heterogeneous impression!

*Anna.* (*Aside.*) Then this wretch is no better than a sarvant.

*Sir Charles.* I am the real Sir Charles Portinscale, who, understanding you always insisted upon your niece resigning her claims with any admirer to you, acquiesced in his scheme, and passed myself upon you as the guide and botanist, to escape your attacks, and have an opportunity of farthering my intentions with your niece. But, Mr. Sample failing to personate the character, I made him acknowledge the imposture, and farther imposed my servant upon you as myself. Your niece has kindly condescended to be mine; and, having an opportunity of declaring myself, I now claim your forgiveness and consent.

*Ver.* Impossible!

*Sample.* Now the whole truth's out.

*Speed.* It is all very true.

*Ver.* Yes, Mr. Botanist, this is a *cryptogamy*,° which I have not seen before, and had no idea of. Sir, you have not my consent, and Lydia will never have one farthing of mine.

*Sir Charles.* My Lydia is herself a treasure of which no fortune can enhance the value. A few months will make her her own mistress; and we need not then be beholden to your consent for our union.

*Ver.* Then my consent is held to be merely ad-scititious.° But, Sir, there are exacerbations of the mind which——

*Speed.* I must again appeal to your amiable forgiving kindness for this second deceit practised against you. But perhaps your Ladyship was not deceived in this instance.

*Ver.* Not a particle more than I was the first time.

*Speed.* May I hope it was myself, and not my assumed title, that gained a heart which monarchs might proudly sigh for?

*Ver.* No, Sir, your insiduous flame——

*Speed.* May I then be permitted to remind you of a bond, which lately, with seductive simpers, you were pleased to force upon me?

*Ver.* Something extremely picturesque in this man and his conduct; he has roughness, sudden variation and intricacy; and if he were not a servant— (*Aside.*)

*Speed.* (*Reads.*) "I, Beccabunga Veronica, of Diandria Hall, do pledge myself to marry the bearer, under forfeiture of all my estate, my *hortus siccus*, sketches and writings. Given under my hand this 21st day of ——."

*Ver.* But you are not Sir Charles Portinscale. I still abide by the forfeiture, if I refuse to marry Sir Charles Portinscale. Now what have you to say?

*Speed.* That the bond is made out to the bearer; and Sir Charles shall exact it as he thinks best. (*Gives it* Sir Charles.)

*Sir Charles.* My Lydia shall dispose of it at her pleasure.

*Lydia.* I have no wish to enforce the penalty. It is yours, Madam. (*Gives it to* Veronica.)

*Ver.* Quite a *capriccio*,° I declare. And so, Sir Charles, you absolutely refuse me?

*Sir Charles.* I cannot accept you myself, and I dare not recommend you to my shadow.

*Ver.* I fear I shall never get another offer half so good, and I'm determined not "to wither on the virgin thorn."° (*Aside.*) He's a vastly clever man, he's a botanist, he's picturesque—I'll throw a Gilpin tint over him. (*Looks through glass.*) Yes, he's gorgeously glowing. I must not view him with the other lights, for a husband should not be either glaringly gloomy, or frigidly frozen; nor should I like to be haunted by a blue devil.—Then he's a servant—but Lord Level married his daughter to a servant. I think the incident would be picturesque; and it would be perfectly botanic for Veronica and Speedwell to marry.

*Sir Charles.* I will answer for his honour, and shall be happy to own him as a relation. I have proved the confidence I place in him, by assigning him the task of being my representative.

*Ver.* But shall not I get laugh—No, a woman in my situation may act as she pleases. We authoresses are privileged people. But how much will my condition be apejorated.° Pray, are you really a botanist? Is it your specific character? or was your botanic knowledge merely assumptuous?

*Speed.* What little knowledge I displayed was really my own, and I hope to better it under your instructions.

*Ver.* A very hopeful scholar, truly!

*Speed.* May I then hope you will marry me?

*Ver.* Marry will I! We will be *connate* like the twin flowers on the same *peduncle*, and I trust our love will be *sempervirent* and *perennial*.° But Mr.——What's your name?

*Sample.* Sample, Miss.

*Ver.* You are an excessively bad practitioner of the mimetic art, you have no artificiality; but as we all seem to be *Dichotamous**, I suppose you will marry my maid and amanuensis, Anna Katharina?

*Sample.* Who caught a mouse, Miss?

*Speed.* I wonder she has not sometime smelt a rat.

*Sample.* Why, I should like her well enough, and, if she'll have a side in my gig, I'll drive her home, and we'll set up a shop for ourselves.

*Anna.* Yes, but I'd rather you'd been a baronet.

*Sir Charles.* But where are the two gentlemen who came as seconds to you and your adversary?

*1st Ped.* Here, Sir. We but undertook the business to prevent any mischief from ensuing. We have succeeded and are satisfied.

*Sir Charles.* May I request to know your names and conditions? Your words do not accord with your outward appearance.

*1st Ped.* We trust, Sir, that we are gentlemen, though thus habited, and taking our tour on foot to gain a knowledge of our country and of mankind.

*Ver.* How fortunate! Pedestrians! How picturesque too their appearance—Another incident for my tour. I beg, Gentlemen, we may be better acquainted. I have often heard of the many who travel in this rational way, but was never before so fortunate as to be acquainted with any. Let me entreat you to be *aggregated* into our party at the inn; and, if I may be so bold as to entreat a slight account of

---

* Branching off in pairs.

your history, to insert in my tour, I shall be particularly obligated to you.—I scarce know, Sir Charles,
in what manner we are to be classed; but as we are so
many *floscules* composing one compound *flos*, I will
pronounce us *syngenecious*, of the order *polygamia
æqualis*, except the Pedestrians, who seem to be as a
*monadelphia*\*.°

*Sir Charles.* All disguise being thus thrown off,
however our follies may be laughed at, I trust that the
adventures of the LAKERS at Keswick will afford an
innocent amusement to those who become acquainted
with them, and that none of us will have any cause
to lament their *denouement.*

## FINALE.

### Sir Charles.

*Happy days are now before us;*
*Let us raise the tuneful strain,*
*Join the full and lively chorus,*
*Antidote to care and pain.*

---

\*  One brotherhood.

### Lydia.

*Though the days we've past were grievous,*
*Yet, when present joy appears,*
*Hope still whispers to relieve us,*
*And the distant prospect cheers.*

Chorus. *Happy days, &c.*

### Speedwell.

*Though Veronica's* Diandria,
*This her class will she forswear;*
*Will she love a single wanderer,*
*Constant to an only dear?*

### Veronica.

*Hitherto, like* CAPRIFICA,
*"Single* wretchedness"° *I've known;*
*My botanic love I like here,*
*And my man I'll love alone.*

Chorus. *Happy days, &c.*

### Sample.

*Will my bonny bale of beauty*
*All her strange vagaries drop,*
*And with me, in bounden duty,*
*Wait upon our retail shop?*

### Anna.

*I had lik'd a man of larning,*
*If with such I could have wed,*
*But an half-loaf I've discarning*
*To prefer to lack of bread.*

Chorus. *Happy days, &c.*

### First Pedestrian.

*We will still, our aim pursuing,*
*For improvement travel on,*
*Men and manners still be viewing,*
*Making all we see our own.*

### Second Pedestrian.

*We not envy power nor riches;*
*We have pleasure, we have health;*
*And experience fully teaches*
*These alone are solid wealth.*

## Chorus.

*Happy days are now before us;*
*Let us raise the tuneful strain,*
*Join the full and lively chorus,*
*Antidote to care and pain.*

THE END.

# NOTES

*Sweet Keswick's vale ....* From John Dalton's *A descriptive poem, addressed to two ladies, at their return from viewing the mines near Whitehaven* (London, 1755), lines 227–32. Plumptre has slightly modified the punctuation and spelling of the passage.

*regular.* Governed by rules, i.e. the accepted canons of dramatic structure.

*Otaheitean.* A native of 'Otaheite', Tahiti.

*make his heroine blue.* In the printed version of his play *The Castle Spectre* (London, 1798), p. 102, Matthew Lewis asserted that he had 'thought it would give a pleasing variety to the characters and dresses, if I made my servants black; and could I have produced the same effect by making my heroine blue, blue I should have made her.'

*Mrs. Mattocks.* Isabella Mattocks, *née* Hallam (1746–1826) was a popular comic actress and singer in the Covent Garden company between 1762 and 1808.

*the other winter theatre.* The Theatre at Drury Lane.

*Mr. Kemble.* Charles Kemble (1775–1854) was one of the leading comic actors of the day: mainly associated with Covent Garden, he acted at the Haymarket during the summer seasons. His brother John was the very well-known Shakespearean actor.

*adapted to the closet.* Suited to private reading.

*Lingo's bad Latin.* 'Lingo' was a character in John O' Keeffe's comic opera *The Agreeable Surprise* (Newry, 1783), first produced at the Haymarket Theatre in 1781.

*consigns it to the closet.* Presents it to the private reader.

*West's Guide to the Lakes.* Thomas West, *A guide to the Lakes: dedicated to the lovers of landscape studies,* and to all who have visited, or intend to visit the lakes in Cumberland, Westmorland, and Lancashire (London, 1778).

*A Journey made in the summer of 1794.* By Ann Ward Radcliffe, the novelist.

*The Botanic Garden.* Erasmus Darwin, *The Botanic Garden; a poem, in two parts. Part I. Containing the economy of vegetation. Part II. The loves of the plants. With philosophical notes.* (London, 1791 (Part I), 1789 (Part II)).

*Cumberland.* George Cumberland (1754–1848) was the author of a number of works on art and landscape, including *A poem on the landscapes of Great-Britain* (London, 1793).

*Mr. Farrington.* Joseph Farington (1747–1821), RA, published his *Views of the Lakes of Cumberland and Westmorland* in 1785.

*the Exhibition.* The Summer Exhibition at the Royal Academy, where in 1798 J.M.W. Turner (1775–1851) had exhibited eight paintings, including some of Lake District scenes.

*Lakers.* To 'lake' was a dialect expression for 'to take a holiday from work; to be out of work', as well as meaning 'to play'. Thus 'lakers' were 'idle persons who love *laking*' (Richard Watson, *Anecdotes of the Life of Richard Watson, Bishop of Landaff* (London, 1817), vol. 2, p. 269). Plumptre's punning use seems to be one of the first times in print that the word (also) denoted those who visited 'the lakes'.

*Sir Charles Portinscale.* Portinscale is a village to the north-west of Derwentwater.

*Bagman.* 'A commercial traveller, whose business it is to show samples and solicit orders on behalf of manufacturers' (*OED*).

*Miss Beccabunga Veronica. Veronica beccabunga* is the improbable Latin name for the plant known in English as brooklime.

*the Queen's Head.* Rebuilt in 1826, the Queen's Hotel and Queen's Head Bar are still to be found in the centre of Keswick.

*Crosthwaite's.* The name of a museum opened in Keswick by Peter Crosthwaite in 1780: apparently Plumptre also knew Crosthwaite's as a hotel.

*green-drake ... palmer-fly.* Types of fly used in fly-fishing.

*Diandria.* The class of plants which have two stamens (male parts), in the Linnæan sexual system of classification.

*Bellona.* Roman goddess of war.

*Vesta.* Roman virgin goddess of hearth, home and family.

*Sociable.* A 'sociable' carriage was one in which four passengers could sit facing one another on two benches.

*hybernaculum.* A greenhouse for wintering plants, or the winter quarters of a hibernating animal (*OED*).

*Morgan Ratler.* A jig tune with bawdy words: it was printed by James Aird in his *Selection of Scotch, Irish, English and Foreign Airs*, vol. 5, (Glasgow, 1797), and the words by W. Goggin in Limerick around 1790. A 'morgan-rattler' was a loaded club, stick or cane.

*voiture.* Vehicle (French).

*pericula.* Danger, peril (Latin).

*riding for Dimity and Co.* Dimity is a type of cotton fabric; Dimity and Co. seems to be an invented firm.

*Ciceroni.* Properly *cicerone* (Italian), 'a guide who shows and explains the antiquities or curiosities of a place to strangers' (*OED*).

*vertu.* Properly *virtù* (Italian): the fine arts or their products.

*the Polish dwarf.* Joseph Boruwlaski (1739–1837), known chiefly through his memoirs, *Mémoires du célèbre nain Joseph Boruwlaski* (in French and English:

London, 1788, 1792), spent much of his life in England from 1781. A sufferer from achondroplasia, his maximum height was 3 feet 3 inches.

*Crow Park.* The park stands to the south-west of Keswick, next to Derwentwater at its north end.

*with a witness.* 'Without a doubt', 'and no mistake' (*OED*).

*ophioglossum*: a small primitive fern; *jungermania*: one of the 'scale-mosses'; *lycoperdon*: the puff-ball fungus or one of its relatives; *polypodium*: any one of a large genus of ferns.

*filices.* The group of plants that includes the ferns (the singular is *filix*). *Felices* (Latin) are fortunate or happy things.

*brozier.* Bankrupt.

*Notitium.* Veronica evidently means 'note', but her word does not exist in Latin.

*auberge.* Inn, place of accommodation (French).

*eleemosynary.* Pertaining to alms or charity.

*getting deciduous.* Falling (deciduous trees are those which shed their leaves each year).

*A non-descript.* An organism that has not been previously described or identified (*OED*).

*It's a tetrandria tetragynia.* Plants of the class *tetrandria* have four stamens (male parts); those of the order *tetragynia* have four pistils (female parts). What follows may be glossed thus: 'The *peduncle* [stalk] is *articulated* [jointed], *membranaceous* [with a membrane], *umbelliferous* [bears umbels, i.e. flower clusters of parasol shape], and *tomentose* [downy]; as are also the *petioles* [leaf-stalks]. The leaves are *cauline* [grow out of the main stem], *petiolated* [stalked], and *lanceolate* [spearhead-shaped]; the *corolla* [inner whorl of leaves enveloping the flower; the petals] is *polypetalous* [has separate petals]; the *calyx* [outer whorl of leaves around the flower; the sepals] is *monophyllous* [joined together]; the *peri-carpium* [seed-vessel] is *tricoccous* [composed of three carpels]; and the *semen* [seed] a *nux* [nut].'

*hortus siccus.* Collection of dried plants.

*the Visionary Horseman.*     Between 1735 and 1745 a 'ghostly army' was reported to have been seen by various observers on Souther Fell (north-east of Keswick); the story was told by James Clarke, who used the phrase 'visionary horsemen', in his *Survey of the Lakes* (2nd edn, London, 1789), pp. 55–6.

*beau idée.* Beautiful idea (French).

*umbrageous.* Shadowy.

*you.* The original has *your*.

*deceptio visus.* Visual deception (Latin).

*mio . . . carissimo.* My dearest (Italian).

*De gustibus non est disputandum.* Concerning taste there is no arguing (or, there's no accounting for taste).

*flags.* Irises (or other aquatic plants).

*"A Shepherd once".* A song from James Cobb, *The Chero-kee, an opera* (London, 1795), first performed at Drury Lane in 1794 with music by Stephen Storace.

*argumentum baculinum.*     The argument of the stick (Latin).

*In filmy, gawsy . . . .* Lines, slightly altered, from Thomas James Mathias, *The Pursuits of Literature* (2nd edi-tion, 1796), part 1, lines 97–100: 'In filmy, gawzy, gossamery lines, / With *lucid* language, and most dark designs, / In sweet *tetrandryan, monogynian* strains / Pant for a *pystill* in botanic pains.'

*monandrian monogynian.* Plants of the class *monandria* have a single stamen (male part); those of the order *monogynia* have a single pistil (female part).

*put on the lion's skin . . . .* An allusion to Aesop's fable of the fox, the donkey and the lion skin: the donkey's ears feature in later versions of the tale.

*costumé.*   Veronica presumably means *costume*, as is printed a few lines later.

*Mr. Daubly.*   Apparently an invention. (Daniel *Daulby* of Liverpool had published *A descriptive catalogue of the works of Rembrandt* in 1796, but he does not seem to have been a painter himself.)

*Syringas*: shrubs of the genus *philadelphus*, including the mock-orange and the lilac; *foliis ovato-cordatis, foliis lanceolatis*: with egg/heart-shaped, or spearhead-shaped leaves; *Cytisas*: a genus of shrubs and trees, including broom and laburnum; *Cestras*: a genus of flowering plants, many with fragrant flowers; *Lycias*: the genus of the box-thorn; *Loniceras*: the genus of the honeysuckles.

*conferva rivularis.*   Obscure; *conferva* was a diverse genus of water-plants.

*coup d'œil.*   Scene (French).

*the owl in the ivy-bush.*   'Like an owl in an ivy-bush' was an expression for an ugly person, someone with untidy hair, or someone who looked 'inanely wise'.

*Enna.*   The region in Sicily from which Proserpine was, according to tradition, carried off by Pluto: Ovid, *Metamorphoses* V, 385–408.

*Coachmakers' Hall.*   The Coachmakers' Hall Society for Free Debate was an important London debating society in the later eighteenth century.

*Archer and Aimwell.*   Two characters in George Farquhar's *The Beaux' Stratagem* (London, 1707), who take turns at pretending to be a lord.

*"speechless messages".*   See *The Merchant of Venice*, I.i: 'Sometimes from her eyes / I did receive fair speechless messages'.

*your royal namesake.*   In 1623 Prince Charles, the future King Charles I of England and Scotland, travelled to Madrid in disguise to seek – unsuccessfully – the hand of of the King of Spain's daughter. See Alexander Samson (ed.), *The Spanish Match* (Aldershot, 2006).

*mesembryanthemum crystallinum.* The 'ice plant', an ornamental succulent with glistening bladder cells.

*Tropæolum.* Properly *tropæolum*, a genus of mostly trailing or climbing herbs.

*caprifica.* The wild fig, which was customarily ripened artificially, by puncturing.

*Collinsonia.* A genus of the order *diandria monogynia*, of plants with two stamens (male parts) and a single pistil (female part).

*Two brother swains.* From Erasmus Darwin, *The Botanic Garden*, part 2 (1789), canto 1, lines 51–4.

*Diœcius.* Of the class of plants which have male and female flowers on separate individuals.

*Vallisneria.* The genus of 'eelgrass' or 'tape grass'. According to a contemporary description the female flower of the 'spiral vallisneria' – an aquatic – rises to the water's surface on a stalk, and there awaits the male flower which breaks from its stalk below the water, rises to the surface, and floats upon the current. (John Hill, *Eden: or, a compleat body of gardening* (London, 1773), p. 195.)

*Katharina ... Kate ... cate.* Cates were bought (as opposed to made) foods, delicacies; the line alludes to *The Taming of the Shrew*, II.i where the same pun is made repeatedly.

*Welsh main.* A match fought between cocks, or more specifically a tournament or 'battle royal' between several cocks in which the fighting continued until a single victor remained.

*chow-chow.* Probably mixed pickles or preserves.

*a devil.* A grilled dish with hot condiments.

*rouing.* Bob probably means 'making a row', though it is possible that 'roving' (in the sense of philandering) is meant.

*faro*: a game in which players bet on the order in which certain cards would appear from a pack; *chuck*: chuck-farthing, a game in which coins were pitched at a mark, and then 'chucked' or tossed at a hole.

*tossing-up.* Gambling on the toss of a coin.

*quizzes.* Peculiar people or things.

*persicaria siliquosa, or noli me tangere.* The yellow balsam, *impatiens noli-tangere*, so called because the ripe seed capsules burst open at a touch.

*Mr. Gray.* Thomas Gray (1716–71), author of 'Gray's Elegy', toured the Lake District in 1769; his 'Journal' of the tour appeared in *The poems of Mr. Gray. To which are prefixed Memoirs of his life and writings by W. Mason* (York, 1775) (his stay in Grange appears on pp. 357–8).

*prevent.* Anticipate.

*Hector.* A swaggerer or bully.

*Geranium batrachoides*: now *geranium pratense*, meadow cranesbill; *flore eleganter variegato*: with elegantly variegated flowers.

*roturier.* Plebian.

*rosa provincialis*: the Provence rose, sometimes identified or confused with the cabbage rose, *Rosa centifolia*; *allium roseum*: rosy garlic.

*ara maculata.* Wild arum, also called cuckoo-pint or 'lords and ladies'. Literally 'maculata' means dirty or tainted.

*Tippoo Saib* (1749–99). Sultan of Mysore from 1782, and involved in various military struggles against the British.

*acumenate.* Sharp, pointed.

*Arm'd in my virgin innocence.* Modelled on lines of Cordelia from Nahum Tate's version of *King Lear* (1681), Act III: 'Bold in my Virgin Innocence, I'll flie / My Royal Father to Relieve, or Die.'

*seeking the bubble reputation at the pistol's mouth.* See *As You Like It*, II.vii: 'Seeking the bubble reputation / Even in the canon's mouth'.

*pass sub jugum.* Go under the yoke: be imprisoned.

*spifflicated.* Confounded, overcome.

*prepensed.* Planned, premeditated.

*cryptogamy.* Cryptogams are plants with no stamens or pistils, and thus no true flowers. Literally a 'cryptogamy' is a clandestine marriage.

*adscititious.* Extrinsic, supplementary: superfluous.

*capriccio.* Caprice (Italian).

*to wither on the virgin thorn.* See *A Midsummer Night's Dream*, I.i: 'withering on the virgin thorn'.

*apejorated.* Made worse.

*connate*: united; *peduncle*: stalk; *sempervirent*: evergreen; *perennial*: (of plants) living for a number of years, (more generally) everlasting.

*as we are so many floscules.* '...as we are so many *floscules* [florets] composing one compound *flos* [flower], I will pronounce us *syngenecious* [united: *syngenesia* is the class of plants in which the stamens are united by their anthers], of the order *polygamia æqualis* [often married, equal: in the class *syngenesia* the order *polygamia* comprises plants bearing inflorescences composed of many florets], except the Pedestrians, who seem to be as a *monadelphia* [single brotherhood: *monadelphia* is a class of plants with hermaphrodite flowers having the stamens united by their filaments]'.

*Single wretchedness.* Probably an allusion to *A Midsummer Night's Dream*, I.i: 'single blessedness'.

Made in the USA
Lexington, KY
08 September 2014